"*The Guards* blew me away. It's dark, funny, and moving—just for starters. With a sharp eye and a lyrical voice, Ken Bruen takes us on a powerful odyssey through the mean streets of Galway, straight into the Irish heart. . . . This is mystery writing of a high order."

—T. Jefferson Parker, author of *Black Water* and *Silent Joe*

"*The Guards* is a wonderful book, wrenching and real, fast, funny, and wise in every sense. Why the hell haven't I heard of Ken Bruen before? He's a terrific writer and *The Guards* is one of the most mesmerizing works of crime fiction I've ever read. . . . This guy is the real thing."

—James W. Hall, author of *Blackwater Sound*

"Ken Bruen is a wonder, and has developed a dazzling style of storytelling—call it White Hot Irish Blues—that sizzles on the page. His novels are gritty, funny, terse, and very, very dark—but also surprisingly compassionate. By far, the coolest books I've read this year."

—C. J. Box, author of *Winterkill* and *Trophy Hunt*

"*The Guards* is raw, hard, bitter, and amazing."

—Jon A. Jackson, author of *Badger Games*

"*The Guards* is an astounding novel. . . . It's so good I can't think of it as a crime novel. It's a fine book with some crimes."

—James Crumley, author of *The Final Country*

"*The Guards* kicked my ass, it's up there with the best. If Elmore Leonard got together with James Joyce to write a Spenser novel, this is what you'd get!"

—David Means, author of *Assorted Fire Events*

for *The Killing of the Tinkers*

"Bruen confirms his rightful place among the finest noir stylists of his generation. This is a remarkable book from a singular talent."

—*Publishers Weekly* (starred review)

Also by Ken Bruen,
published by The Do-Not Press
The Hackman Blues
The White Trilogy:
A White Arrest
Taming The Alien
The McDead
London Boulevard

Other books by Ken Bruen:
Funeral
Shades of Grace
Martyrs
Rilke on Black
Her Last Call to Louis McNeice
The Guards
The Killing of the Tinkers

KEN BRUEN

BLITZ

or... BRANT HITS THE BLUES

 St. Martin's Minotaur ⚞ New York

To Joe and Gertie Dolan

www.minotaurbooks.com

ISBN 0-312-32726-9
EAN 978-0312-32726-2

First published in Great Britain by The Do-Not Press Ltd.

First U.S. Edition: June 2004

10 9 8 7 6 5 4 3 2 1

PART ONE

*Privacy is the first luxury
of the rich
and the final dignity
of the poor.*

Ferdinand Mount, *TLS*, March 2001

THE PSYCHIATRIST STARED at Brant. All round the office were signs that thanked you for not smoking.

The psychiatrist wore a tweed jacket with patches on the sleeves. He had limp, fair hair that fell into his eyes, thus causing him to flick it back every few seconds. This doctor was convinced he had Brant's measure.

He was wrong.

Said:

'Now, Sergeant, I'd like you to tell me again about your violent urges.'

For the interview, Brant had dressed down. Beaten bomber jacket, blue jeans on their last wash, a pair of Dockers he'd bought in New York. He hadn't shaved and this gave his granite face a blasted sheen. Now, he reached in his jacket, extracted a pack of Weights and a Zippo. The lighter was as worn as Brant but barely legible was the inscription:

'1968'

Brant, smiling at the memory, cranked it. A cloud of smoke rose.

The doctor said,

'Sergeant, I must insist you extinguish that.'

Brant took a particularly deep drag. The type that

sucked your cheeks till you resembled a skull. Blowing out, he said,

'And you'll do what exactly if I don't... arrest me?'

The doctor sighed, made a note on Brant's chart. He was using a heavy, gold Schaeffer, proud of its splendour, said,

'This doesn't help your case, Sergeant.'

Brant smiled, said,

'Nice pen.'

'Oh?'

'Yeah, it says a lot about you.'

In spite of himself, the doctor asked,

'Oh, really? Pray tell.'

'That you like a solid phallic symbol in your fingers.'

Almost rising to the bait, the doctor managed to rein in, said,

'Sergeant, I'm not sure you realise the gravity of your situation. My report will be a major factor in whether you remain in the Force.'

Brant shot to his feet, startling the doctor, leaned over the desk, said,

'You're a little jumpy there, Doc.'

'I must insist you re-take your seat.'

Brant moved closer, one knee up on the desk, said,

'Thing is Doc, if I get bounced, I'm fucked. This is the only work I can do. So, if I'm out, I'm sure I'd lose it big time and do something truly reckless.'

The doctor, as part of his internship, had spent six months attached to an asylum for the criminally insane.

He'd gone eyeball to eyeball with some of the most dangerous people on the planet.

Up close and almost personal.

None of them had scared him the way Brant's eyes were
scaring him now. He stammered,

'Are... are you threatening... me...?'

Brant seemed to consider, appeared to back off, looking
almost sheepish.

Almost.

The doctor, sensing victory, near shouted,

'I should think not.'

Then Brant lunged, nutted him. The top of Brant's head
connecting with the bridge of the doctor's nose, back he
went, chair and all. Brant swung down off the top, came
round the desk, pulled open a bottom drawer, said,

'I knew it!'

Pulled out a bottle of Glenfiddich, two glasses.
Grabbing the doc by the lapel of his jacket, he pulled him
up, righted the chair, said,

'Get a grip, for fuck's sake.'

Poured two hefty wallops, shoved a glass into the doc's
hand, said,

'Get that down you.'

The doctor did.

The booze hit him almost as hard as the nut. Brant
poured an even greater dose, said,

'Now you're cooking.'

The doctor, born to an upper middle-class west London
family, educated at the best schools, had never been physi-

cally struck in his life. As President of the Cambridge Debating Society, he'd flirted with verbal aggression. But among his own kind. In the asylums of his training, he'd had the backup of:

Brutish orderlies

Restraints

Straitjackets

And, of course, the ultimate leveller – Thorazine.

Sure, driving his Bentley, he'd experienced mild road-rage and a woman, behind the safety of her windscreen, had once even mouthed,

Wanker.

Delicious thrill.

Now, he was in psychic shock, took the second drink like an automaton, drank it down. Brant stretched over, fixed his tie, straightened his lapels, said,

'Sure, look at you, you're a new man.'

He let himself out of the office without a backward glance. He'd left the Glenfiddich, perched centre desk, the cap on the blotter. The receptionist smiled and Brant said,

'He's asked not to be disturbed for the next hour.'

She gave an understanding nod, said,

'Poor lamb, he works too hard.'

Brant considered asking her for a ride but she looked the deep type. She'd have issues and want to talk after.

He hated that.

❐

Outside, he went to a phone kiosk, rang CIB. The police who police the police, bottom feeders. Brant said:

'Could I speak to DI Crest?'

'Speaking.'

'Sir, I hate to rat out a fellow officer...'

Brant knew what was coming.

'It's not ratting out. We're all on the same side. CIB are not the enemy, so you're only doing your duty.'

'That's how I see it, sir. Doctor Hazel, our shrink... he's drinking on the job. Even as we speak, he's sloshing malted like a wino.'

'And your name, officer?'

'PC McDonald.'

And he rang off. The kiosk, of course, was awash with hooker advertisements. Every service available to man or beast. One:

> 'Madam with whip expertise
> requires strong male for
> disciplinary lessons.'

He liked the sound of that, could hear the theme of *Rawhide* in his head. He jotted down the details with his newly acquired, heavy, gold Schaeffer.

PC McDonald had attempted to shaft Brant on more than one occasion. When word got out that he'd shopped Hazel – and word always got out – McDonald would be shunned. As Brant put the pen in his jacket, he said aloud,

'Cap that.'

There was a sense of things gone stale – the half trays of doughnuts and cakes, the air in the living room where people had been smoking all day. During the morning and early afternoon there'd been a quiet and communal air of both grief and love, but by the time Dave got back, it had turned into something colder, a kind of withdrawal maybe, the blood beginning to chafe with the restless scrape of chairs and the subdued goodbyes.

Denis Lehane
Mystic River

THE DAY ROBERTS' wife died, he was getting a bollocking from his Superintendent.

Like this.

The Super, nibbling on a rich tea biscuit, said between bites:

'Brant is for the high jump.'

'Sir?'

Roberts' managed to inject just enough cheek to pass muster.

'And I blame you, Roberts.'

'Yes, sir.'

'How many times did I tell you to reign him in?'

'Many... many times... sir.'

Now the Super caught the tone, shouted:

'I don't care for your manner, laddie.'

'No, sir.'

That's when the phone rang. The Super snapped up the receiver, barked:

'What?'

The expression on his face changed and he glanced at Roberts, said,

'I see.'

He didn't.

Roberts felt ice along his spine.

The Super said,

'Take a seat, Chief Inspector.'

The use of the title warned Roberts it was going to be rough. The Super pulled open a drawer, a replica of the one belonging to Brant's doctor. Even the bottle was a twin. And of course, the requisite two glasses. He poured near Irish measures, pushed one across, said,

'Drink that like a good man.'

Roberts did. He didn't want to ask, wanted to postpone whatever was coming. The whiskey kicked like a mugger. Warmth invaded his stomach. The Super said,

'There's been some bad news.'

'Oh?'

'Your wife...'

The Super couldn't recall her name so plunged on.

'She's been in a car accident.'

'Is it serious?'

'She's dead.'

Roberts stared at his empty glass. The Super leant over, added a fresh jolt. Roberts asked,

'How did it happen?'

'She was rear-ended in Dulwich. Killed instantly.'

Roberts walloped down the drink, shuddered and said,

'Maggie Thatcher lived down the road.'

'Excuse me?'

'Yeah, she put property values through the roof. My mortgage is a killer.'

Then, realising what he'd said, he gave a bleak smile.

The Super stood, said,

'We'll get you home. Your son will have to be told.'

'Son?'

'Yes, your boy?'

'I have a daughter.'

''Course you do, my memory is not the machine it was. Let's get you going, eh?'

While not quite being the bum's rush, it was in the neighbourhood. The Super came round the desk, put a hand around Roberts' shoulders. Roberts said,

'I could go another round of that malt.'

'Better not, laddie. Alcohol on an empty stomach and all that.'

Roberts got to his feet, staggered, said,

'I never liked her, you know?'

The Super wanted him out and now, said,

'It's shock, Chief Inspector, you don't mean that.'

As roaring alcohol does, it turns nasty as quick as benevolent. Belligerence clouded Roberts' face and he near shouted:

'Listen up, you prick. Christ, you're so used to barking orders, you never hear anybody. I loved her, I just never liked her.'

The Super, stunned at the verbal attack, tried not to react, said in the voice 'the manual' suggested for such circumstances:

'I'm going to forget that last outburst. We'll put it down to trauma.'

A knock on the door. The Super said,

'Come in.'

PC McDonald, gorgeous as ever, entered. He took, as Woody Allen says,

'Handsome lessons.'

He was the Super's new hatchet boy. Though from Glasgow, he managed to convey the culture of Edinburgh. That is, he'd ironed out the creases so his accent resembled Sean Connery's burr. Recently, his carelessness had nearly cost WPC Falls her life. He knew that Brant knew that. More than ever, in collusion with the Super, he hoped to shaft:

Brant

Roberts

Falls

The Scottish Tourist Board.

The Super said,

'Constable, please see to it that the Chief Inspector gets home and stay with him.'

'Yes, sir.'

Inwardly he sighed. Babysitting that git did not come into his plans. He led Roberts outside, where a Volvo was waiting. Roberts said,

'A bloody Volvo!!

'Car pool is tight today, sir.'

Got Roberts in the back and slid behind the wheel. Adjusted the mirror so he could get a good look. Didn't much stomach what he saw. A dowdy officer, looking like he'd done a month's night duty on the Railton Road. Roberts asked,

'Got a cigarette?'

'Don't smoke, sir.'

'Me neither, but what the fuck has that to do with anything?'

I don't know what all the fuss is about Fred Astaire's dancing. I did the same thing, in high heels and backwards.

Ginger Rogers.

PC FALLS WAS attempting to re-touch her roots. Not her hair, her heritage. Reared in Brixton, she'd been proud of her colour.

Black was beautiful.

...and she'd begun to lose it.

Chip

      Chip

           Chip

                 Away.

The foundations of her confidence had eroded. Not without reason. The death of her father, the loss of a pregnancy, suicide of her best friend, indebtedness to Brant and her flirtation with alcoholism.

Who wouldn't be hurting and badly?

She was.

Of all the loss, in truth, she most missed herself. At a recent knees-up Brant, in his bastardised Irish fashion, had played Van Morrison. That Belfast dude knew about ghettos. She'd been mesmerised.

Brant had said,

'Van's the man.'

'Might be.'

But Brant knew he'd struck a chord. Gave her the wolf

21

smile, all teeth and malevolence. Thus she'd bought *Astral Weeks*. In an attempt to re-black, she'd bought:

Strictly 4

My Niggas

Me Against the World

the huge selling platinum albums by Tupac Shakur. Then, on the news, she'd seen teenage members of The West Side Boyz Militia with '2 Pac' on their T-shirts. She checked him out and found that he'd been a hot actor and was murdered after a Mike Tyson fight in Las Vegas. In Brixton Market, she'd bought a framed picture of him to put on her shelf. Wasn't doing the job though.

Recently, she'd taken the Sergeant's exam. Brant had said, 'You're a shoo-in. The fucks won't flunk a black chick.'

Chick!

Mind you, it was nothing compared to names he'd called her in the past.

She failed.

A WPC from Asia passed so *The Guardian* wouldn't be revving up. What Falls had done was call Porter Nash. An openly gay sergeant, he was her new best friend. He'd answered with:

'Yell-o.'

'Porter, it's Falls.'

'Hi, hon.'

'I failed the exam.'

'The bastards.'

'Can you help me?'

'With what, hon?'

'A night out.'

'Done deal.'

'Thanks, Porter. I want to get legless.'

'Like tequila?'

'Love it.'

She'd never had it.

'There's a pub near Warwick Square, right by Paddington Station called The Sawyers Arms. Meet you there at eight.'

She visualised the map, then,

'Porter!'

'What?'

'That's west London.'

'So? You need to circulate.'

She injected whine and cred into her voice, an impressive feat, said,

'It's not my manor. *Wot dey say to a black girl from Brixton?*'

He laughed, a warm sound, said,

'It's Paddington, they do black.'

Reverting to her own voice, she said,

'But they do to blacks... what?'

'My bleeper's going, dress hot... we're clubbing.'

Click.

When he'd been assigned to her nick, word preceded him. His rep was good: 'street cop', the best recommendation. But larger than that, he was gay; that he'd risen to sergeant was a bloody miracle. The day of his arrival, graffiti appeared on the toilet walls.

Porter Nash sucks cocks

In the gents and ladies.

What the liberals term 'Informed discrimination'.

Yeah.

The canteen was jammed for the first coffee break. No one was going to miss this. Even Gladys, the tea lady, was a-tingle. When Porter arrived, a hush fell. He'd gone to the counter, got a tea and two sugars. What the cops called 'a Sid Vicious'. They'd all seen *Sid and Nancy*. Gary Oldman, wrecked on every chemical known to man, shouts at his record company rep, who had asked what he wanted:

'Cup a tea, yah cunt... and two sugars.'

Gladys admired Porter's courtesy. His lovely voice, saying:

'Please.'

And wonders, 'Thank you'.

She said to her husband later,

'Say what you like but them 'nancy boys' have lovely manners.'

After Porter had his tea, he stood and moved to leave. All eyes on him, he turned at the door, said,

'Even I'd draw the line at blowing Brant.'

Stunned silence.

Then rapturous applause and howls of approval.

He was in.

One of the best things about being 42 rather than 14 is that you don't spend your life in a constant sweat about how scary sex and men are.

Julie Burchill

THE ARRANGEMENTS FOR Mrs Roberts were fast and cheap. Roberts was in serious financial shit and had settled for a Croydon cremation. The most expensive item was the urn. Brant had driven him over there. No other officer attended, mainly because they weren't told. Even Falls had got the message:

'You're not welcome.'

The crematorium was a nondescript building near the Mecca Bingo. As Brant and Roberts entered, a couple were coming out with their urn. Brant said,

'Business is brisk.'

Roberts didn't answer, a wave of nausea hit him and he put out a hand to touch the wall. Brant got him a chair, produced a hip flask, said,

'Get that down yah.'

He did.

It burned like a bastard. He said,

'I don't know can I go through with this.'

'You'll be okay, it's over in jig time.'

'You think I should have gone for a burial?'

'No, it's all the same deal. You're saving a few bob, she'd be glad.'

'My daughter wouldn't come.'

'Smart girl.'

'She's shacked up with an Asian guy in Coldharbour Lane.'

Brant knew a great joke involving curry but felt he might hold on to it. A man emerged from an office, approached, said,

'We're ready for you, Mr Roberts.'

They entered a small room. There was a row of pews and what appeared to be a miniature assembly line. A coffin was placed on it, near smothered in white roses. Roberts asked,

'Who got the flowers?'

Brant near smiled, said,

'Guy on the stalls in Streatham owed me a favour; does a clean line in the fruit and veg.'

In fact, he'd also sent over a dozen pineapples but the crematorium caretaker had had those away. A tape began to play; it sounded like a Welsh choir-gone-boy band. Obviously well used, as it skipped in parts, startling the listener. Brant said,

'Me, I like a nice Moody Blue.'

The attendant began to remove the flowers and signalled: 'It's time.'

Brant nudged Roberts, said,

'Couple of last words, guv.'

Roberts couldn't move so Brant led him over, took his hand and placed it on the coffin. The wood felt warm. Roberts tried to speak but no words came. Brant said,

'We'll miss you, love.'

And they stepped back.

A muted whirring and the casket began to move. A steel shutter opened in the wall, a red glow momentarily visible, then the coffin was gone. Tears slid down Roberts' cheeks. Brant took his arm, said,

'We'll wait outside.'

The attendant showed them into an office and withdrew. Brant produced the flask, said,

'We'll get legless today.'

Roberts nodded, drank deep. Brant produced his packet of Weights and the Zippo. Cranked up. His brand of cigarettes were getting harder to find. Now he had to travel to the West End for them, ordering a month's supply each visit. The proprietor had said,

'You'll need to change, soon they'll be unavailable.'

Normally, Brant leaned a little on shopkeepers. More out of habit than need. But West End guys answered to a different drummer. He'd taken his supply, paid in full. Boy, he hated to shell out top whack for anything, felt it blunted his edge. He'd have to find an angle on this guy but hadn't found it yet. Not unduly worried, sooner or later he got them all by the balls. Roberts said,

'Gimme one of those.'

'Sir?'

'Come on, Brant, one cigarette won't kill me.'

'They're kind of strong, guv.'

'Give me the bloody thing.'

Brant fired him up, expecting Roberts to erupt in a fever of coughing and spittle.

Nope.

After a time, the funeral director approached; he was carrying an urn, solemnly, in both hands, said,

'Mr Roberts, your wife.'

Roberts had the hysterical impression he was being introduced, wanted to shout:

'How can I greet her? She's no bloody hands.'

Brant, that extra sense – as always – attuned, said,

'I'll take that.'

The director whispered:

'There's the matter of... ahm... the bill.'

'We are The Bill.'

A slight titter from the director, though he was far from amused. The burn-and-bury business will smash that right out of you. He said,

'Things proved a tad more costly than anticipated.'

Brant led him to a corner, said,

'You gave a price, got paid, and now you're upping the ante, shaking down the dead?'

'It's the unforeseen extras, how they do mount up; every enterprise is prey to them.'

Brant gave him the look, asked,

'You know what enterprise I'm in?'

'Of course... sergeant.'

'Trust me pal, you don't want to fuck with me.'

Now Brant gave him the smile; it reminded the director of the corpses, before they'd been made up. He said,

'I see.'

'I bloody hope you do, pal.'

Then he rummaged in his jacket, found some crumpled change, said,

'Bit of a drink in it for you, eh?'

The director turned frosty, said,

'I don't drink.'

'You fuck with me again, you'll wish you did.'

❒

They got a minicab to Camberwell. The driver, from Rawalpindi, got lost twice. As they got out, Brant said,

'On me, guv.'

He leaned into the driver, flashed his warrant card. The man sighed, said,

'Not even a tip?'

'A tip is it? Here's one, buy a flogging *A to Z*.'

They got seriously wasted in a pub frequented by the staff and patients from the Maudsley Mental Hospital, formerly known as the infamous Bedlam. Sometime during the evening, they lost the urn. Or one of the patients nicked it.

Either way, Mrs Roberts was history.

*In the early 1980s, a member of the notorious
Dunne drugs family was led away in handcuffs.
Just before he got into the prison van, he turned
to the pack of reporters, said,
'If you thought we were bad, just wait till you
see what's coming next.'*

Paul Carson
Evil Empire

BARRY WEISS WAS seriously pissed off. He'd had a market stall at Waterloo. Then the local beat cop had brought the VAT crowd down on his arse. Finished that enterprise. A traffic cop burned him for drunk driving and he'd lost his licence. A neighbour reported him for excessive noise and a black policewoman read him the riot act. Coming home from the Cricketers, he'd taken a piss against St Mark's Catheral.

Guess what?

A blond fuck of a Scottish cop named McDonald did him for public indecency.

He'd had it.

At the arse end of East Lane, he bought a gun from some non-European fuck for fifty quid. A Glock, who hadn't heard of those babes? Lightweight, reliable, sleek. He loved that piece. To celebrate, he shot a traffic warden in Balham, like anyone gave a toss. It wasn't even reported in the *South London Press*. That he found seriously depressing. Who the hell did you have to shoot to get a review? He'd failed to score any charlie the past few days so you do what you can. Bought a bottle of vodka and six cans of Red Bull. The working stiff's cocaine.

It was starting to happen, a nice buzz building and Iron

Maiden on the speakers. Crank it up. Then it hit him: kill a
cop. It was what Oprah called a light-bulb moment. No...
no, hold on a mo'... kill lots of cops. And if he got caught?
There'd be book deals, Sky News, mini series'... And
fuck... hold the phones... Jerry Springer. Where was the
downside? Fucked if he could find it.

Dressed to kill: Nikes, Manson T-shirt (Charlie, not
Marilyn), black 501s, black bomber, Glock. Nine in the
evening, his brain electric, he went out. Darkness coming
fast, he hit the Oval tube in five minutes flat. There, outside
the pub, a policewoman doing up her tunic. He strode up,
capped her, kept moving. On the Northern Line in six and
out on Clapham Common in 15 minutes. Adrenalin
surging up beyond the booze, heading to Nirvana, whis-
pering: 'I'm a player'.

❏

Barry was a good-looking guy, or so two women had told
him. Okay, so they were hookers, but didn't that count?
He was twenty-eight, six-foot in height, weighing in at
close to two hundred pounds. Not a guy to fuck with. Few
did, except for the police who seemed to fuck with him all
the time. He had brown hair, shaved to a No. 1; gave his
scalp a blond polished appearance. Blue washed-out eyes,
a hook nose and a stab of a mouth.

He'd been a regular at a gym in Streatham and could
bench impressively. A unisex joint, he liked to ogle the
women in their spandex. What he'd do was oil all over, get
the sweat rolling and flex the pecs. If the women noticed,

they hid it well. A gay had come on to him in the saunas and he'd slapped him up the side of the head.

Slapped him hard.

That was all he sang.

Barry liked to read, but only crime, especially true crime. Had them all:

Ann Rule

Joe McGuinness,

Edna Buchanan

Jack Olsen.

He'd studied these books. Sociopaths, psychopaths, serial killers, he couldn't get enough. For him, those guys rocked. Focusing on their profiles, he found total identification. Bundy, Gacey were his role models. Their lives fascinated him, how they took it all the way. No fucking hostages, like never. Barry's lucky number was eight so he decided to kill that number of cops.

Years ago, a particularly brutal one had given him a hiding. Outside a pool hall in Peckham, Barry had had one too many Supers. He'd gone upstairs and was giving it large to some Pakis over table number three. The cop had arrived.

Alone.

Barry had said,

'Fuck off, pig.'

Turned to accept the approval of the pool punks. An almighty blow landed, rocking him from the crown of his head to the tip of his arse. Sprawled him across table ten. He couldn't believe it – the cop had flattened him with a cue. What about procedure, civil liberties? Didn't anyone read the fucking liberal newspapers? Then he was turned over and the pool ball jammed into his mouth, the cop saying,

'It's Sergeant Brant to you, fuck face.'

Grabbed Barry by the seat of his pants and pulled him down each painful step of the stairs. To roars of approval from the Pakis. On the street, he was bundled to his feet, the cop saying,

'Here's where I put me size nine up your arse.'

And did.

The shame, the humiliation, plus the task of ejecting the ball from his mouth, Barry hadn't been back to that hall since. He'd bashed some Pakis though, every chance he got. Brant was the pinnacle of his list. When he'd killed the initial seven, he'd go for Brant with something spectacular. Made him hot just planning it.

Sometimes I think I know what it was about and how everything happened. But then, I shake my head and wonder. Am I remembering what happened or what other people think happened? Who the hell knows after a certain point?

Frank Sinatra

SOME YEARS BACK, Brant had had the hots for the late Mrs Roberts. All that tight-ass Dulwich snobbery got him cooking. He'd caught her in bed with a young stud, did what he did best:

blackmail.

In return for saying nothing, she had to go out on a date. Brant got suited and booted, took her to a flash joint in Notting Hill, surprised her with his charm. Just as she felt her interest quicken, he was summoned away to a particularly Peckinpah case. The fall-out got him knifed in the back and he'd left her alone after that. An A-list villain had taunted Roberts about his Sergeant shafting the missus. One drunken night, Roberts asked him straight out if there was any truth in the story. Brant answered,

'Aren't we mates, guv?'

Managed to slide a sneer and a whine into the question.

The evening after the crematorium, Brant came to muttering,

'Yeah, mates!'

His hangover was a classic. Big, roaring and merciless, he spotted remnants of green chicken under a chair, prayed:

'Don't let me have eaten that.'

Stomach lurch and he was on his knees over the toilet bowl. After the upchuck, as he cleared the tears from his eyes, he saw he had indeed eaten the green. The phone rang and he shouted,

'Fuck off.'

It didn't.

He snapped the receiver, growled,

'What?'

Super Brown, who said,

'Sergeant Brant, where on earth have you been?'

'Giving succour to the Chief Inspector, as ordered, sir.'

'Well, get your botty over to the Oval, an officer is down.'

'Sir?'

'On the double, Sergeant.'

Click.

Holding the dead phone, Brant said,

'Botty?'

FALLS HAD DRESSED to impress. Okay, so Porter Nash was gay, and this wasn't like a date. But you never knew where an evening might take you. She wore a white sheath and gasped at how black her skin appeared, said,

'Yo' looking foxy, girl.'

She was.

Two stud pearls for that Essex effect; keep the punters confused, get them thinking,

'High yaller.'

Then, a moment, what would Rosie say? Not anything, not any more. Her best friend, a white cop. Then an HIV junkie had bitten her and she'd killed herself. The loss washed over Falls anew.

Rosie's pig of a husband had said – regarding the funeral arrangements:

'No police, thank you very much, and especially none of those vulgar wreaths in the shape of helmets.'

Falls had thought then and still did: Fuck you, asshole.

Sent the biggest, most ostentatious one she could get. Shape of a big, blue, Met helmet. Now, she went to the cabinet, took out a bottle of scotch, said,

'Just a tiny one, get me stoked.'

She'd had some problems with booze, okay, so it had

39

been said she'd a major problem. Like, it killed her father and she hadn't the money to bury him. Three large. God, the mortification; phew-oh, Brant came through with the readies, said,

'You owe me, Falls.' He collected... and not financially. To make it worse, he'd saved her from the Clapham Rapist. Christ, she'd never be free of him. The way he liked it. Drank the scotch fast, it hit like love, warming artificially and ruefully. She thought: Just as artificial.

Cynic that.

Rosie, white girl as she was, used to play Leonard Cohen. Falls would chide,

'Girl, yo' want to hit de blues? Lemme git you Nina Simone.'

A line of Leonard Cohen's shifted itself from her grief... something about the future and about it being murder.

Got that right, Greek boy.

She caught a number 36 bus, rode the top deck as far as Paddington Station, the booze bubbling in her blood. The conductor was a brother, said, near sang,

'Sho' looking fine.'

She smiled and he pushed,

'Yo' all wanna drink after mo shift?'

Gave him the full Railton Road glare, he backed way off.

The Sawyers Arms was a halfway decent pub. Mix of navvies, travellers and trainee yuppies, not the worst. Porter had the corner table, drinks all set. He stood, said,

'You beauty.'

Gave her a big hug, that turned some heads, like she gave a rat's, said,

'Let me see you.'

He stepped back, wearing a suede tan jacket, open white shirt, navy chinos, police shoes. But the guys always did. She said,

'*Baaaad* jacket.'

'From Gap.'

'Whatever.'

They were full delighted with each other, she lifted her tiny glass, sniffed, made a face. He said,

'Tequila slammer.'

'And you?'

'Scotch.'

They touched glasses, drank deep, he reached in the jacket, took out Menthol Superkings and a chunky lighter, she said,

'Mixed metaphor.'

He loved that, said,

'I love that. The menthol is for the light-on-your-feet brigade and the lighter is for the whole YMCA gig.'

She wasn't sure she got all that, but who cared? His mobile phone went, she said,

'Don't answer.'

'I'll have to.'

He did. Listened, his face clouding. Said,

'Okay.'

Turned to face her, said,

'Officer down.'

Perhaps we unconsciously avoid situations for which we are ill-equipped, even if avoiding them entails an amount of immediate suffering.

Dervla Murphy

OUTSIDE THE PUB, Porter said,

'I've transport.'

Falls gave him a look, said,

'You told me we were going to get legless.'

'So?'

'So how come you brought wheels?'

Porter hung his head, said,

'I hadn't thought it through.'

She didn't believe him, said,

'I don't believe you.'

'Okay, Falls.'

'Okay? What the hell is okay?'

'I wasn't going to drink much.'

'But you were going to let me drink lights out.'

'Yes.'

They'd reached a red Datsun he'd indicated was it. He said,

'This is it.'

'The poof-mobile.'

That stung but he rode it out, got the car in gear and she asked,

'What sort of mate is that?'

'What?'

'You heard me. We go for a night out and you're planning to be Miss Prim.'

He swerved to avoid an Audi, let down his window,
shouted:

'Get some driving lessons.'

She looked at him, regretted again he was gay, said,

'You sounded like Brant.'

He grimaced, said,

'Nobody sounds like Brant.'

He got a break in traffic, cut across a black cab, got
some serious speed on. Both of them were thinking of the
fallen officer but neither wanted to mention it. He said,

'I'd have had a few drinks.'

'Forget it.'

'I'm sorry.'

'What did I say? Didn't I just say forget it?'

He took a deep breath, said,

'It's a WPC.'

Falls stared out the window, then said,

'Is she dead?'

'Yes.'

'Fuck, fuck, fuck.'

Porter knew about the suicide of Falls' friend. For her
the death of a WPC was doubly hard. He said,

'I didn't get any more details.'

'She's dead, what more is there?'

' I mean... you know... her name... or what happened.'

'We'll know soon enough.'

They were coming up on Waterloo. Falls said,

'I used to live here.'

'Yeah? What was that like?'

'Shite.'

He laughed then stopped abruptly, feeling guilty. She asked,

'You've had some of these?'

He knew she meant police deaths but pretended not to follow, asked,

'Some of what?'

'Officer down.'

'Yeah, a few.'

They were coming up on Kennington Road, could see the mess of blue lights ahead. Porter said,

'The word is out.'

Police cars were everywhere, causing chaos. Any motorist complaining got short shrift. It was not a night to worry about public relations. A traffic cop flagged down their car. As Porter opened the window, the cop said,

'There's no way through, you're going to have to wait.'

It wasn't a request, it was an order. The cop's face was grim, his eyes saying, 'Give me lip and I'll have your ass.'

Porter produced his warrant card; the cop examined it closely, said,

'Sorry, sarge, I thought you were civilians.'

He grabbed an eyeful of Falls, the sheath dress, her legs, asked,

'New uniform?'

Porter let it hang a moment then,

'Watch your mouth.'

The cop, taken aback, muttered,

'Just kidding.'

Porter was out of the car, in the guy's face, going,

'An officer is down and you're kidding?'

Falls was behind him, said,

'Porter, come on.'

Porter looked at his car, then back to the cop, said,

'I'm leaving this vehicle in your hands. I'll expect it to be well cared for.'

The cop indicated the chaos building from all directions, groaned,

'Aw, sarge.'

Porter had already turned away, was marching towards the Oval. Falls shouted,

'Wait up!'

As she caught up, he said,

'When I was stationed at Kensington...'

'You were stationed at Kensington?'

'Yes, a sergeant there, named Carlisle, one of the best cops I've ever known....'

Falls was thinking: Carlisle, Porter Nash, no wonder they got a west London gig. He continued,

'I was taking a lot of flak over being gay, he took me aside, said,

"Front the bastards up".'

'What did he mean?'

'Don't hide who I am, put it right in their faces, let them deal with it.'

'Did they?'

46

'Some... the point is, he showed me it's about being a copper, all the rest is irrelevant.'

'He was white, hetero?'

'Yes.'

'Easy for him to say then.'

Porter rounded on her, fire in his eyes, near roared:

'He was decapitated in a high-speed chase. The driver of the stolen vehicle was fourteen. You think it mattered then what colour Carlisle was, or what his sexual orientation was?'

They'd reached the Oval; a canopy had been erected near the station. Falls said,

'They'll have her in there.'

Porter said,

'Wait here.'

And he approached the officers standing outside the station.

Falls heard a low whistle, turned to face Brant, he said,

'That is some dress.'

Brant looked shocking, as if he'd been on the booze for a week. She said,

'You look shocking.'

'I've been consoling the Chief Inspector.'

'How is he?'

Brant stared at the canopy then back to her, said,

'Fucked.'

I spit in the black ash and rub it between my
fingers and my palms and then I take the ash and
draw a cross upon my face
A cross to keep the fear away
A cross to keep the fear—
A cross to keep—
A cross.

David Peace
Nineteen-Eighty

THE DEAD POLICEWOMAN was Sandra Miller. Not even a south Londoner; originally from Manchester, she'd come to London two years before. Spent six months in telephone sales, drove her demented. She'd applied to Ryanair and the Met Police, figuring one way or another, she was going to fly. The cops replied first, then Ryanair. What she did was compare the uniforms. Decided the police had a slight edge. Plus she relished the expression on people's faces when they asked,

"And what do you do?"

Being a glorified waitress on a cut rate airline didn't have the same impact. Found she enjoyed being a WPC.

Assigned to South-East District, she got a bedsit in Camberwell and set about policing them streets. She'd been on the job a year when Barry had randomnly selected her for death. Two shots and her life was done.

The Super had appeared at the scene, as did every cop for miles around. To make sure your face was seen. A horde of uniforms had been despatched to canvass residents of buildings overlooking the crime scene and beyond. Brown was talking to detectives when Brant appeared. Brown tried to disguise his loathing for the Sergeant, said,

'I'm busy here. You'll be briefed in the morning along with everybody else.'

To his surprise, Brant didn't move; stood there with that habitual smirk. The Super snapped:

'Was there something?'

'Yes, sir.'

'Can't it bloody wait? This is a murder inquiry.'

Brant stared at the traffic, then turned, said,

'There's a witness.'

'What, why wasn't I told?'

'I've been trying to tell you for the past half-hour but your...'

He moved his arm in a definite gesture of contempt to indicate McDonald.

'... driver said you were busy.'

The Super saw the detectives around them suppress a smile. He tried for authority, asked,

'Why hasn't this... witness come forth earlier?'

'Nobody asked him.'

'What?'

'Nobody spoke to him.'

With that, Brant nodded to a man standing near the kerb and he approached. If the heavy presence of police intimidated him, he wasn't showing it. He had the air of a street person, knowing, crafty, ready. The Super inspected the witness. Obviously not impressed, he barked,

'You say you saw the shooter?'

'Yeah.'

'Describe him.'

The guy gave the hint of a smile, took a moment, said,

'Looks like him.'

He was pointing at McDonald. The Super near lost it, shouted,

'That's a damn policeman!'

'He had the same hair, blond and cut tight, you know, like a nancy boy or somefink.'

'And what were you at, hanging around on a street corner, you just happened to see the shooting?'

The man was unfazed by the Super's shouting, said,

'I sell *The Big Issue*.'

'What's that supposed to tell me?'

The man pointed to the Oval tube entrance, said,

'That's my patch; every day, morning till night, I see what goes down.'

Now the Super turned to Brant and ordered,

'Get him down to the station and take a full statement.'

The man didn't move, asked,

'What about my customers? This is one of my busiest times, the pubs will be closing soon. People have had a few, they get that guilt going.'

'You'll be compensated.'

'Yeah, like I believe that.'

❐

Brant took the guy to the pub, asked,

'What will you have?'

'Pint and a large brandy.'

He got a pint. They took a table at the rear; Brant said,

'It's Tony, right?'
'Anthony, and you're Brant?'
'You know me?'
'Fuck, who doesn't ?'
'So, run the description by me.'
'Aren't you taking notes?'
And got the look.

❐

The area was preserved at the Oval, scene of crimes had been and most of the cops had drifted away. Porter asked Falls,
    'You want to get a nightcap?'
    'No.'
    'Hang on, I'll get the car, drop you home.'
    'I'll walk.'
    'Come on, Falls, you can't walk home like that.'
    She rounded on him, temper flashing.
    'What's wrong with the way I look?'
    'Jeez, nothing, but you know… a woman on her own.'
    Her hand on her hips, she said,
    'I hope some asshole tries, I really do.'

❐

McDonald was feeling better. The day had started badly; he'd arrived at the station to find a dead rat pinned to his locker. Then, in the canteen, he'd moved to join a group at a table and, to a man, they'd gotten up and left. As the day progressed, he realised nobody was talking to him. Finally he'd approached the duty sergeant who glared at him. He asked,

'Sarge, what's going on?'

'Like you don't know.'

'Sarge, I swear, cut me a bit of slack. What did I do?'

The sergeant was a Scot, otherwise he'd have blanked McDonald. He looked round, ensured no one was listening, said,

'You shopped the Doc.'

'Doc... what Doc?'

'The one you're seeing, the shrink. You called CIB, dropped him right in it. They went over there, found him pissed as a parrot, trying to get his leg over his nurse.'

McDonald tried to get his mind in gear, said,

'I wasn't seeing any shrink.'

The sergeant raised his eyebrows, said,

'Whatever, the shrink is fucked. Won't be a consultant to the force no more. Nice little earner, I hear. The word on you is you're a fink, a rat.'

McDonald had suddenly realised, said,

'Brant.'

'What?'

'He's behind it; he made the call, I know it.'

The sergeant leant forward, cautioned,

'Whoa, laddie, you're in deep enough. The last thing you need is to have Brant on your case.'

McDonald was offended, countered,

'I'm not afraid of that bastard.'

The sergeant took a deep breath, said,

'Everybody else is.'

'Yeah, well.'

He felt he'd over-emphasised his case, tried to with-draw, said,

'Anyway, I'd appreciate it if you could spread the word that I'm not a fink.'

The sergeant was shaking his head, went:

'No three ways to Sunday, you're fucked.'

How do I know all this? Because I'm crazy, you can always trust the information given you by people who are crazy; they have an access to truth not available through regular channels.

Norma Jean Harris

THE CALL CAME to the main desk of *The Tabloid*, was re-routed to the Chief Crime Correspondent, a man named Dunphy. He picked up, said,

'Yeah?'

'I have information on the police killing.'

'Let's hear it.'

A pause, then Barry said,

'Have some fucking manners.'

Dunphy sat up straight, recognising a tone, asked,

'What?'

'I'm offering information, you don't even say hello.'

'Hello.'

'That's better.'

'I'm glad you're happy.'

Another pause, then:

'I'm not fond of sarcasm. Maybe I'll start on journalists when I finish my cop quota.'

Dunphy hit the record button, eased his voice a notch, said,

'We got off on the wrong foot, let's start over; what did you say your name was?'

'Jesus, what a corny ploy. I'm not sure you're up to the task.'

'Task?'

'Yeah, reporting from inside the cop killings.'

'You're a cop?'

'Ah, you're too fucking dumb.'

Click.

Dunphy lit a cigarette, a light sweat on his forehead, knew he'd screwed up. He was about to listen to a replay when the phone rang, he grabbed it, said,

'Yes?'

'One more chance.'

'Great.'

'And learn some manners.'

Manners weren't Dunphy's strong point but he could fake it, as he did most things. He tried,

'I appreciate your calling.'

'Where are you on the food chain?'

Dunphy wasn't sure what this meant, said,

'I'm not sure what that means.'

'Do you have any clout, are you one of the movers and shakers?'

'Oh… I run the Crime desk.'

'I can make you famous.'

Now he desperately wanted to let some obscenities fly; instead, he said,

'That would be good.'

'Which do you prefer… seven… or eight?'

He knew better than to ask 'what' so he went with,

'Seven.'

'Seven it is.'

'May I ask, seven what?'

'Seven more cops to kill, bye.'

Click.

Dunphy ejected the tape, headed for the editor's office, wanted – after all these years – to shout:

'Hold the front page!'

Barry came out of the phone kiosk, power was surging through his system, he couldn't believe the rush, went:

'Fucking hell.'

He'd had a journalist grovelling, actually had the guy kissing his arse and this was only the beginning. The thing to do now was to show he was serious. The gun was hidden in the waistband of his jeans, tucked against his spine. Like in the movies. Well, this was his movie and he was going to give them *Acopalypse Now*, not to mention *Redux*. A police panda car was parked at the beginning of Camberwell New Road. Just the driver. Barry paused, waited to see if there was any sign of a partner.

Nope.

The window was open, the officer listening to the radio. Barry took another look around, as is mandatory in Camberwell. If a cop car parks, everybody legs it, it's almost the law. Barry wanted to play, said,

'Yo' there, policeman.'

The cop turned, gave him the full stare, asked,

'You want somefink?'

Barry snapped back:

'Thing!'

'What?'

'You said somefink... You think you'd at least be able to speak properly.'

The cop was debating getting out, had his hand on the handle, said,

'Piss off.'

Barry registered shock-horror, said,

'Oh my God! Is that any way to develop public confidence in the police?'

The cop narrowed his eyes, said,

'I won't tell you again. Get lost.'

'But I have a question.'

'What question?'

'What would you do if I called you a cunt?'

Before the cop could get out, Barry said,

'Ah... just as I thought.'

And shot him twice in the face.

Turned to walk quickly across the road, managed to jump on a 36 bus and in five minutes, he was in the centre of Peckham. Caught another bus from the opposite direction and felt the rush as the bus came towards the panda. A crowd was swarming and by peering down, he could see the policeman's cap on the ground. He thought: Shit, that would have made a brill trophy.

All the crime books were big on trophies.

I found a kind word with a gun more effective than a kind word.

John Dillinger

THE PAPERS WENT ape:

Cop Killer Terrorises City

Madman Menaces Met

Second Police Execution

Superintendent Brown lashed his officers. He'd taken a bollocking from early in the morning as even the Home Secretary called. He was determined to pass it along. Brant was at the back of the briefing, sipping a large Starbucks. Porter Nash glanced at him and got a wink. Brown was winding down, said,

'Due to the recent death of his wife, Chief Inspector Roberts is on extended compassionate leave. As you are all too well aware, we have a scarcity of senior officers due to the current crisis worldwide. In view of this, we are promoting Sergeant Porter Nash to acting inspector and temporary head of the inquiry.'

The room was shocked, even Brant was paying attention. A hand went up and Brown said,

'Yes?'

'Shouldn't we promote from within?'

The Super glared at the questioner, added his name to the shit list, said,

'The powers that be have decreed we need perspective

61

on this one. Already we are the focus of a media circus. As acting Inspector Nash arrived from the prestigious…'

He paused, biting the words, letting the implication wash over them, before continuing,

'…West London Branch of our glorious Met, he'll satisfy the demands for the professional policing we seem to lack here in our primitive South East Division.'

Spontaneous applause.

Save Brant, who was staring openly at Porter. They both knew the immediate meltdown of this. Porter was Brant's superior. Brant thought: The Super's finally shafted me; just bent me over and did it.

He half-admired the nastiness of the scheme. Plus, a gay in the driving seat was the ideal scapegoat.

West London that.

In the canteen, Brant sat in a corner, lit a Weight. No one approached till Porter arrived and asked,

'Get you something?'

'Ah.' Brant took a deep breath, before continuing, 'A Sid Vicious and two Club Milks. I think my sugar level's dropped.'

Gladys, as always, was delighted to serve the poof, and ventured:

'Might I congratulate you on your… elevation?'

'Thanks, Gladys, but it's only a temporary position. I'm sure Chief Inspector Roberts will return soon.'

She put her hands on her hips, said,

'That fellah's away with the fairies… oops… oh-my-God, I didn't mean anything. No offence.'

Porter smiled and she admired his teeth. If only straight men would devote such energy to their appearance. She was becoming hot for the pillow-biter.

He said,

'Two teas, sugared; oh, and two Club Milk biscuits.'

Gladys fixed a malevolent eye on Brant, said,

'You be sure that devil pays for his own.'

'I will.'

As he walked away, she whispered,

'Mind your back.'

Then bit her tongue; probably not an appropriate caution for a nancy boy.

Brant wolfed down the Club Milks, rolled the wrappers in a ball, bounced them off a new recruit's head then turned to Porter, said,

'Sorry, would you have liked one?'

'I don't do sweet.'

Brant enjoyed that, said,

'Must put that in my notebook. Something you learnt in Knightsbridge, no doubt.'

'Kensington.'

Brant sucked his tea, as if he were draining it past his gums, answered:

'What?'

'I was in Kensington not Knightsbridge.'

'What's the fucking difference?'

'A lot if you own Harrods.'

Porter took out his kingsize Menthol, knew the effect they'd have on Brant, asked,

'Got a light?'

He did.

Brant didn't rise to the bait and Porter learnt a little. He knew the fearsome rep. Rumours of Brant's playing vigilante, taking bribes, bugging the Super's office, messing with Roberts' wife, losing a suspect at Heathrow, his near-death from a knife in the back. He asked,

'Are you as black as you're painted?'

At first he thought Brant hadn't heard, was about to repeat the question when the eyes locked on his, asked,

'Are you as nancy as they say?'

Porter finished the cig, said,

'Touché. The thing is, are we going to have a problem?'

Now he got to witness the full neon of Brant's smile, but no trace of humour or warmth. Brant said,

'We already have a problem, a sick fuck is killing police officers and he's just started.'

'I meant, between us.'

Brant stood, brushed crumbs from his jacket and said:

'I know what you meant. I'm not your thick Paddy, least not always. Problem? Not unless you follow me into public toilets. Hadn't we better move our arses, at least look like you know what you're doing.'

Porter got up, thinking he'd made a total mess of the 'let's get it all out in the open' crap. He did realise that whatever went down, 'open' was not a terrain on which Brant operated.

Dancing
With
Jack
D

THERE'S A TERRIFIC book on death by Bert Keizer called *Dancing with Mr D*.

It's a cracker.

After Rosie's suicide, Falls had tried to find some sense to the act. As she'd torn through the literature of grief (and she'd discovered a thriving industry there), she'd found only this book was of any help.

That and Jack Daniels.

Pour that sucker over ice and you didn't even need the books. Falls, after the Porter night out, had decided on a night in. Take a long Radox bath, the old scruffy bathrobe, a takeaway pizza and who'd be hurting? She'd had the bath, got the robe on, when the doorbell rang.

'Fuck,'

she said.

Answered it... to a Hitler Youth.

A few years back, she'd found a young skinhead scrawling 'Nazi' on her wall. He'd spelled it wrong. She'd given him the price of a cup of tea even as the term 'black bitch' rolled in his mouth. An unlikely friendship had begun. Over the next few months she'd lent him books, music, money. He didn't mention to his cronies of this tainted affair. It was a long time before he even gave his name. Or rather, his nickname. A Saturday evening, he'd drifted over; there was never an 'orchestrated arrangement', he showed or he didn't. He'd asked,

'Can I watch the football?'

'Sure.'

'I didn't bring nothing.'

'You drink beer?'

'Course I do, whatcha' implying? I'm not a bleeding pooftah.'

Falls enjoyed him immensely. His blend of front and fragility stirred a feeling she didn't even bother trying to analyse. Taking a six-pack of Amstel from the fridge, she said,

'I thought you might be a cider man.'

As always he searched her face for a sign of ridicule. What he saw was a lovely woman, real prize and almost forgot her colour.

Almost.

Later she heard him roar as the game finished, asked,

'Who won?'

Suspicious, he near jeered,

'What do you know?'

'Leeds against Man U... right?'

'So?'

'Was Ian Harte playing?'

'He's a wanker is what he is.'

And Falls was delighted anew. She loved his predictability. In her mind, he was her project. Turn him, you could turn anything, anyone.

Dream on.

She'd finally got his name.

'Metal'.

Falls laughed out loud. Blitzed on beer, he'd finally told her. Realising by his furious face that she'd fucked up, she tried to rally, went:

'I'm not laughing at you, I'm laughing with you.'

She knew how weak that was. He was on his feet, spittle on his lips, shouting,

'But I'm not laughing. You see me laughing?'

A takeaway pizza – heavy crust – and more beer eventually calmed him down. That plus her '2 Pac' T-shirt. Wait till he discovered the dude was black; he thought it was an ad for beer. She'd asked gently,

'So, how did you get... such... an *unusual* name?'

''Cos.'

'Yes?'

'I used to be a headbanger, like heavy metal, I'd get a blast of glue, go mental.'

'And now?'

He shrugged, began,

'Since I joined the British National Party...'

Stopped.

To gauge her response, couldn't detect a dial tone, continued,

'I stopped all that shit.'

She pulled the tab on a beer, handed it over, said,

'Now you stomp people.'

'Only wogs. And Pakis. Pooftahs sometimes.'

Now she was answering the door to him, dressed as a
Hitler Youth. She asked,

'What?'

'Can I come in?'

'Not in that garbage.'

He glanced round nervously, bit his lower lip, said,

'I'm in trouble.'

'Come in.'

She moved to the window, folded her arms, waited.

He finally spoke:

'Can I get a brewski?'

'No. What did you do?'

He began to pace, then,

'I think we killed a geezer.'

She went out to the kitchen, got the Jack, two mugs,
brought them out. He eyed the bottle, said,

'Rocking.'

She said, 'Sit down.' And felt like his mother.

Poured large wallops, handed a mug over. His mug bore
the logo:

'Marsha Hunts'... Men'

He said he and a 'unit' had been patrolling Vauxhall.
Falls asked,

'Looking for bovver?'

He stared at his boots. Doc Martens with reinforced
steel toe-caps. He gulped down the drink, near choked,
sputtlered, then said,

'Just keeping it safe for white blokes.'

Now she was leaning over him, said,

'John – oh yeah, I know your name and your thick file from Juvenile Records – it's ball-busting time... you ever foul my home with any more racist shit or name-calling, I'll make you eat those Doc Martens.'

Metal was afraid; she seemed to have completely lost it, a hardness in her eyes like granite. She slapped his head, asked,

'Who'd you hurt?'

'A sand nigger... sorry... an Arab-type guy.'

'How bad?'

'He wasn't moving.'

He got his tobacco, began to roll a cig. She snapped,

'Don't you smoke in my house.'

He slipped the gear back into his pocket. Falls' face was creased in concentration. Then:

'Okay, I'll look into it—'

'Thanks, I...'

'Shut up, I haven't finished. If the man is dead, you're on your own; in fact, I'll nick you myself. Go home and wait till you hear from me.'

He stood up and she added,

'It's choice time, John. If you haven't killed this time, you'll either quit them Nazis or quit coming here. Do you follow?'

'Yes, ma'am.'

As he went out, he asked,

'Are we like... you know... still mates?'

'I don't know.'

Shut the door.

I have two ways of acting...
with
or without
the horse.

Robert Mitchum

BRANT HAD A new snitch, the life and blood of any police force. In his time, Brant had met some beauts. One way or another, they'd all come to a nasty end. One memorable Cypriot guy had been literally kebabbed to death. It had put Brant right off lamb souvlakis. His latest was old for the trade. Just over sixty, he'd been in nick for thirty of those years. His name was Radnor Bowen. No one knew if this was his actual name but as his speciality had been break-ins on Radnor Walk, it could have gone either way. Thus the severity of his sentencing; judges don't like scum from 'south of the river' to get notions.

He was tall and thin, with open, warm eyes. You'd take him for a kindly uncle and he'd take you for everything you'd got. He'd been trying a new career until Brant had decided to run him.

Radnor was aware of Brant's rep, plus the knowledge that his predecessors had come to a bad end; he was determined to outsmart the Sergeant. They met in an Irish pub off the Balham High Road. This time Radnor had got there first, was nursing a half of bitter. It tasted like warm piss, a potion he'd been forced to drink on his first stretch. He looked round the huge saloon, posters of the Wolfe Tones abounded. A framed picture of 'The men behind the wire'.

72

Coming attractions were advertised on the walls and these included tribute acts to:

Daniel O'Donnell

Brendan Shine

Dale Haze and The Champions.

He shuddered – the originals were horror enough. An ashtray on the table contained the words:

'Players Please'

He wondered if it was an omen. You don't spend half your life in stir without acquiring superstitions. He was wearing a Crombie overcoat, silk cravat, blazer, grey slacks and highly polished black shoes. The barman had him clocked as ex-army. The pose of ramrod-stiff back was a further legacy of prison.

He knew what Brant would want. The cop killer, the whole south-east was buzzing with rumours. Radnor intended to make this his jackpot, a payoff that would take him to a small cottage in Cornwall and safety. The door opened and Brant strode in, looking as feral as ever.

Brant marched over to the bar, got a scotch and had some words with the barman. No money changed hands. Then he came over to the table. Brant was wearing a semi-respectable suit and a Police Federation tie. He asked,

'Been here long?'

'Just arrived.'

Brant got his cigs out, fired up, said,

'You'll know what I want.'

'I do.'

'So, spill.'

Radnor focused, said,

'I'm on to something.'

'What?'

'I need paying.'

Brant smiled, dropped his cig in the bitter, said,

'Oh, sorry.'

Radnor gave a sad smile, didn't answer. Brant leant over, asked,

'What had you in mind?'

'Serious money.'

'Whoa... like retirement benefit?'

He let his hand rest on Radnor's knee, said,

'Bony fucker, aren't you?'

Is there an answer to this, an answer that bears some relation to sanity? If there is, Radnor hadn't got it. Brant began stroking the knee, said,

'But you don't have the brains of a chicken... do you?'

Then Brant twisted his fingers and jolts of pain shot through Radnor's thigh, along the testicles to lodge in his gut. Tears ran from his eyes as Brant continued,

'I doubt if you've any Irish blood in you, you're an out-and-out chap, the English gent in your poncy cravat and fucked coat. Me now, I've a wild streak of the Celt, makes me unpredictable. Them Irish, did you know they invented kneecapping? Answer me.'

'Ahm, no, yes... I guess one would surmise... '

'Ah, shut up with your fake Hampstead accent. As I was saying, kneecapping, it's a nasty business. They fix you up as best they can, but you always have a limp. How does that sound, "Radnor the gimp". How does that go down in your retirement package?'

Brant looked at the barman, said,

'Yo, innkeeper, a brandy and port and a large scotch before closing time.'

Then he grinned at Radnor, all teeth, no warmth, said,

'Christ, decent help is hard to find, know what I mean? Here's what we'll do: have a nice stiff drink, fortify our resolve, maybe a pack of ready salted or are you a cheese and onion man?'

Radnor managed to croak,

'Cheese and onion.'

'Good man, that's the ticket. Barkeep, a selection of your freshest crisps, no expense spared.'

A man entered, took a stool at the bar. Radnor checked him out of professional habit. Brant did the same. The barman arrived with a tray of crisps and the drinks, put it down in the centre of the table. Brant said,

'Well, go on Rad, pay the man.'

Radnor had to dig deep, produced a note and Brant said,

'Keep the change.'

Sly smile from the barman. When he got back behind the counter, he said to the man on the stool:

'Get you?'

'A pint of lager and something for yourself.'

Bigger smile from the barman, the day was improving by the minute. Brant raised his glass, said,

'Okay, tell me.'

Radnor took a deep breath, felt he was moving through a minefield, said,

'There's a guy who's been shouting his mouth off; he was in that poncy gym at Streatham, beat a homosexual half to death there. When the management had a word and mentioned the police, he said: "I'll be giving them something to worry about very soon".'

Brant stopped mid chew, crisps lodged in his teeth, said,

'That's it?'

'The guy is a nutter.'

'Fuck, if we pulled in every wanker who said that, we'd be up to our arse in suspects. What's his name?'

'I don't know. I'm meeting up with a guy who'll give me that.'

Brant stood up, said,

'Don't bother, I'll go the gym, ask the manager.'

Radnor, his dream evaporating, pleaded,

'Don't I get something?'

'You've got cheese and onion... what more do you want, you greedy bugger?'

And he was gone.

At the bar, the man had been watching them. The barman said,

'That's a cop and his snitch.'

'Yeah?'

'Yeah, that piece of garbage that left, he's Brant, a total pig; and the git in the cravat, he's flogging him information.'

The man looked impressed, said,

'You seem pretty sure.'

'I'm the boss, it's my job to know.'

He tapped his nose with his index finger.

Barry Weiss studied the man who'd remained and con-templated offing him but decided against it. He'd a full programme. Instead, he said to the barman,

'Like another?'

Illusions can make you jump to conclusions.
Like off a bridge.

Andrew Vachss
Sacrifice

PORTER NASH HAD spent the day organising the teams. Officers tracked down every lead, went door to door, compiled a list of police haters. This last job was massive, and it had had to be narrowed down to a workable size. He finally got home at midnight, put a vegetarian meal in the microwave, zapped that. Tore off his work clothes and put on an old judo outfit from his days of aspiration. He took a large bottle of Evian from the fridge, drank deep. Could feel a slight relaxation at the base of his skull.

Porter lived at Renfrew Road in Kennington, opposite the old police training college. There was some neat irony in that but he hadn't the time to infer it. The apartment was spacious, he had the entire top floor. Painted white, it had expensive, comfortable furniture, state-of-the-art music centre, mega TV, the works. An alcove had been siphoned off to hold his computer, printer, neat stacks of paper.

Now, he selected Puccini, turned it on low, enough to dance along his senses without serious involvement. The microwave pinged and he removed the meal. He'd bought a stash of these at Selfridges. Sat at his wooden table, prepared to eat. His doorbell rang, took him by surprise. It crossed his mind to get the police special from underneath the bed but as he had no sense of peril, decided to act on that. Opened the door to Brant, said,

'Sergeant?'

'Evening all. Not disturbing anything, am I?'

Porter gave him the full stare. Brant was dressed in a boilersuit, a very dirty one, as if he'd been crawling through a dumpster. Maybe he had. If half the stories were true, he actually lived in one. Brant raised an eyebrow, asked,

'Going to ask me in?'

'I was in the middle of a meal.'

'Go ahead, I'd some spare ribs earlier, stuck in me teeth.'

Porter stood aside, watched as Brant took in the apartment and heard him say,

'The Japs have a word for this... this type of bare look, don't they?'

Porter coming behind, was impressed, said,

'Yes, minimalist.'

'Shite was the word I'd in mind.'

And Porter eased a gear, seeing how easily Brant engaged you then, wallop; he'd have to remember that. Brant was wrinkling his nose, not an easy task, asked,

'What do I smell, that stuff the hippies use?'

'Patchouli oil.'

Brant gave a knowing smirk, said,

'To cover the "wacky baccy", eh? Doing some of the weed are we, a little recreational drug use?'

Porter didn't bother to answer, moved to the table and stared at his cold dinner. Brant at his elbow asked,

'What the hell's that? Jeez, you need to get some meat in you, a thick juicy steak, get the blood flowing.'

Porter moved to a chair and Brant asked,

'Don't I get a drink, first time to your pad and all that?'

'In the bottom press, help yourself.'

Brant hunkered down, pulled the door to reveal a range of spirits, went,

'Fuck, no wonder you stay home. Hit you with anything?'

'No, I've some water here.'

Brant splashed some Armagnac into a heavy crystal glass, took a deep gulp, said,

'Wow, that kicks.'

Porter could feel his eyes closing, watched Brant continue his tour, pick up a book, read:

'*This Wild Darkness*; *Diary of My Death*. Who the hell is Harold Brodkey?'

'It's an account of his death from Aids.'

'A fag, eh?'

'Does it matter?'

Porter had, despite his resolution, allowed a note of testiness to tinge his tone. Brant was delighted, said,

'Mattered to him. Me, I only read McBain. I saw him once, in the distance, wish I'd spoken to him. Tell you what, I'll lend you one, get you away from this morbid shit.'

Porter shook himself, said,

'Nice as this chat is... is there a point?'

'I need your advice.'

'Advice?'

He was truly surprised. Brant said,

'I don't care about you being a pillow-biter. Fuck, I don't give a toss what people do, long as they keep it the fuck away from me. But I respect you, there's not many I do.'

Porter was up, moved and poured a scotch, a large one, took a sip, said,

'What's the problem?'

Brant drained the glass, seemed to retreat, a baffled look in his eyes. Then, as if summoning all he'd got, he focused, said,

'I'm losing it.'

'In what way?'

'I'm blanking out. Not often but enough to be worrying. I don't want to talk, eat... not even drink. It takes a huge effort to drag myself out of bed.'

He stopped, unsure how to continue, so Porter asked,

'What do you want to do?'

'Stare at a wall, do nothing, absolutely nothing.'

Porter put the glass down, chased his cigs, lit one, blew out a cloud of smoke, said,

'It's burn-out.'

'What?'

'You're on meltdown; a couple of days doing nothing, you'll start to come back.'

'You sound pretty sure.'

'I am, I've been there.'

'You?'

'Sure, I was fucked nine ways to Sunday.'

Brant's turn to be surprised, he looked at the futon, sat down carefully, as if it might bite, said,

'I don't read you as a guy who gets frazzled.'

Porter paused, held a finger up as Puccini hit 'Viena la Sera', whispered,

'*Bimba dagli occhi pieni di malia.*'

'What?'

'The next piece, it's my favourite.'

He paused, then:

'Two years ago, we'd a paedophile on the loose, luring kids into his car at Holland Park. We knew who he was but couldn't catch him in the act. The kids were too traumatised to identify him, plus he was connected. A showbiz agent, he had heavy juice to call on. The guys at the nick, they classed me on a par with him... because of my sexual orientation. Put used condoms in my locker, sugar in the petrol tank... the usual stuff.'

Porter took a deep breath.

'I was under massive pressure, chugging valium, mainlining caffeine, smoking again, anyway, I took things into my own hands. Broke into the creep's house, four in the morning, mashed his privates with a baseball bat. A time later, I was burnt out, took a leave of absence, hid in my house and right after, I got transferred.'

A sound disturbed him, louder than the music. Brant was snoring, his head back on the up-rest, mouth open, dribbling spit. Porter got some blankets, covered him, said,

'Goodnight, sweet prince.'

I wake frightened now; it is a strange form of fright – geometric, limited, final.

Harold Brodkey
This Wild Darkness

PC McDONALD, STILL hurting from being cold-shoul-
dered by his colleagues, had begun shadowing Brant. He'd
been surprised to find him enter the building at Renfrew
Road. Was he seeing a woman, checking out a lead...
what? He called the Super. He'd been warned:

'This is my private number, if you call me, it better be
good; unless you have Brant's balls, don't call.'

Now the Super said,

'McDonald!'

'Yes, sir.'

'I'm due at the Regional Dinner in ten minutes, this had
better be vital.'

'Sir, I've followed Brant to a flat in Renfrew Road but
I've no idea who he's here to see.'

He could hear spluttering, choking, indignation writ
huge, then,

'You bloody half-wit, you called me for that?'

'I thought it might be a break, sir.'

'Porter Nash lives in Renfrew Road, don't you know
anything? And sonny, what's this I hear about you ratting
out a doctor?'

McDonald looked at the phone, wanted to scream at
the Super, say:

'And what am I doing for you, eh? What do you call this?'

He said,

'Sir, it's a setup.'

'Nobody likes a fink, especially a fink who gets caught. Am I making myself clear?'

'Yes sir, absolutely.'

Click.

McDonald rummaged around in the glove department of his car, found some mints, popped them in his mouth. He wished he still smoked but was determined to get ahead. Cigarettes were for the likes of Brant. As he sucked on the mint, he took a small camera from his pocket, shot off a few of Porter's building. With any luck, he'd get Brant and Porter in an embrace, fix them both.

Porter was eating muesli when Brant stirred. First thing of a morning, he was not a pretty sight. He stretched, reached for a cigarette, retched violently. Porter prayed he wouldn't vomit on the futon, asked,

'Don't you want some breakfast?'

'Coffee, two spoons, no sugar.'

When Porter brought it, Brant scratched his arse, asked,

'Did you interfere with me?'

'Yeah, right.'

As Brant slurped at the coffee, Porter asked,

'Any idea who we're looking for?'

'A nutter, hardest type to catch. I checked out a gym in Streatham yesterday, got the name of a guy who might be worth a visit.'

'You want me along?'

'No, you're lead: you're up to your eyes in bullshit.'

Brant shook himself, stood, said,

'I'm off.'

'Yeah, well, don't be a stranger.'

Brant looked at his shoes, then:

'What I was saying last night...'

'Stays with me.'

A pause, then:

'I was just tired.'

'Sure, grab some shuteye.'

As Porter let him out, Brant said,

'The other thing...'

'What?'

'About you being a good cop.'

'Yeah?'

'I meant it.'

'Thanks.'

As he moved down the hall, Brant added

'For a pooftah.'

Porter shut the door.

Outside, Brant stopped, looked up at the building. McDonald started clicking; he'd swear there was a look of longing on Brant's face. Blown up in stark black and white, Porter's address in block letters on the top, it would tell its own story.

After Brant had gone, McDonald waited.

Twenty minutes later, Porter was down and McDonald nailed him. A little creative editing, the two men could be united in print. Nice big poster on the notice board, call it 'Hands-on policing' maybe. McDonald felt better than he had for a long time.

Dan Fante used to say he was a compulsive writer because his strength came from being an insane drunk. On being asked why he quit drinking, he answered:

The voices in my head were trying to kill me. One in particular, I called it Jimmy. Jimmy was truly a dangerous motherfucker. I had three suicide attempts behind Jimmy. As for therapy, I've been Rolfed, Re-birthed, even done Reichian Therapy and that's just the Rs.

BARRY WEISS WAS having a mixed day. He'd won a prize, that was the up-side. Every month, he bought *Bizarre* magazine: man he *loved* that sucker. Gathered all the weird and crazy shit, put it between glossy covers and was seriously deranged. Interviews conducted by people with names like Billy Chainsaw – Barry loved that dude. The most whacked-out letter each month received a bottle of absinthe. Barry had written six times... Nothing.

Then bingo.

Postman knocked early and there it was, he'd won. Unwrapping the parcel, he punched the air, shouted,

'*Bizarre* rules!'

This was his letter:

'I'm writing from Fraggle Rock, the name for the Psych. Ward in Brixton Prison. *Bizarre* was given to me by a six-foot-two transvestite who's here for attempting to mug a Tory backbencher. Her name is Miranda. I think I'm developing a crush, a bottle of absinthe would definitely improve our relationship.'

And he'd given his own address as a 'care of'. He was so

up on the win, he had a slug immediately, knocked him flat on his arse, and he said,

'That is the bollocks.'

The bad news was, he was out of ammunition, went:

'How did that happen?'

On the fingers of his left hand, he counted:

'Okay, let me see here: the traffic warden, one bullet; the woman cop, two or three?'

He couldn't recall, continued,

'The guy in the patrol car, two?'

Truth was, Barry had been drinking since lights out, hammering the vodka in. A car boot sale on Clapham Common, some Ukranian guy was selling rip-off Stoli in batches of six. Barry wasn't altogether sure whether he'd killed anyone else. He hated to have to alter his modus operandi. The serials he admired, they'd all had a signature. Discontinuing the Glock was unprofessional. Still, he'd call the newspaper guy, tell him he was making the deal more personal. He'd rented a locker at Waterloo Station, put all the stuff connected to the killings in there, just in case he got rousted. His beloved crime books, he gave to the Salvation Army 'cos he hated those fucks.

Suddenly thought: A hammer!

He had one; a solid, heavy job. It meant getting up close. Aloud he shouted:

'Moving to Defcon One!'

SERGEANT CROSS LIVED in a studio apartment at Sirinham Point. Nineteen floors of crap with a view of the Oval Cricket Ground if you lived on the west side, floors eleven to nineteen. Cross had his on the second floor, east side. What he got to watch were nuns. Right opposite was a convent. If there's a stranger place for them, Cross couldn't think of it. There was a huge statue of some saint just inside the gate. Saturday nights – post football, post pub – the statue got to wear a Millwall scarf. Once, it had been a Man-U trophy. He had been tempted to climb the gates, have it away. But there were rumours of guard dogs in the grounds.

Nuns and Rottweilers: urban living in the zeitgist.

Cross had seen the Mother Superior once and figured they didn't need the dogs. He had been married and – par for the course with the job – was divorced. His kids hated him and the settlement was crushing the life out of him. He was lucky the council gave him a push up the waiting list. Now, but two months from retirement, he was keeping a low profile. He went to work, volunntered for nothing and kept his mouth shut. When he got out, he had a job lined up with Marks and Spencer. Want to talk cosy number? Bust rich Arabs and receive praise for it. Cross was delighted to be leaving. Christ, they had a faggot heading up the murder inquiry. And the streets! Crack cocaine had opened the deluge and every bargain-basement chemical was out there. He couldn't even keep track of the names. Recently, he'd been told of GHB, said,

'You mean like grievous bodily harm?'

Laughed in his face. It was liquid 'E', all the joys of ecstasy and no payback. Like there was ever such a drug. If he'd learned anything, it was payback. Every bloody thing cost and there was no free ride.

Ask the nuns.

He'd asked Brant who explained 'Gamma Hydroxy-butyric Acid', said it usually ended in coma. Brant had asked:

'Ever hear of River Phoenix?'

'No, where is it?'

'It's a person, was a person, a young actor. What's with you? Don't you watch movies?'

'Just westerns.'

'Well, they say that drug killed him.'

Cross would have been more impressed if John Wayne had been the victim. Brant had sighed and walked away. No matter what stories he heard about Brant, and there were always new variations, Cross liked him. He was the old-school type copper: thick, ruthless, fearsome.

And he'd do you a favour. When Cross moved into Sirinham Point, Brant had patched him into a cable TV line. Cross had moaned,

'Jeez, sarge, I don't think I can afford that.'

'Nobody can, you won't be getting any bills.'

'How come?'

Brant had stared right through him, asked,

'You really want the answer?'

Pause.

'No, I suppose not.'

'Thought not, couple of weeks, I'll fix up all that digital crap too.'

'I owe you, Brant.'

'Join the queue.'

The one passion of Cross's diminishing life was Sky Sports. With the big screen, he'd sit there all day, a six-pack, cod 'n' chips, some saveloys for variety and how content could one man be? He was a Leeds supporter, going all the way back to Norman Hunter. He wasn't too happy about Robbie Keane but relaxed when they bought Fowler. It was four on a Thursday afternoon, he was eating fried bread topped with mayo when his bell went. As he approached the door, crust in his mouth, he asked,

'Who is it?'

'Cable guy.'

◻

Afterwards, even Barry would concede that 'it got away from him'. Sure, he'd intended to bash the guy – why else had he brought the hammer? – but he'd lost it big time, really did a number on the poor fuck. Talk about overkill. Bits of brains on the wall, in Barry's hair. He said aloud:

'Now, that's bizarre.'

Had started out well enough, the cop had let him in, seemed nervous about 'being billed'. Barry had decided to play a little, replied,

'But you are The Bill.'

...And set off the cop's antennae. Barry blamed the absinthe, stuff made you whacko. He saw the light go in the eyes and had to quickly swing the hammer.

Missed.

Bloody fucking fresh air and Cross had rabbit punched him but hadn't fully connected.

Else...

Of all the dumb luck, the fuck had tripped on the carpet as he prepared to pummel Barry. No more screwing around. Barry, hurting from the punch, was on him, screaming:

'My bloody neck, you could have killed me!'

Raining blows on the guy's face, lost in a Technicolor blur of blood and fragments. Till a banging on the ceiling snapped him out of it. With revulsion, he'd jumped away from the mess beneath... And, okay, threw up.

DNA that.

What else could Barry do? He'd have to torch the whole building. Teach the fuck above to pound on a person's ceiling. In the kitchen, if an alcove could be called thus, Barry finished the fried bread. Said,

'Mayo... what's that about?'

Found the beer and a massive thirst, drained two cans, in, like... jig time. His clothes were ruined, he couldn't possibly leave in them. Went through the cop's meagre wardrobe and settled for a police jacket, the all-weather black job. Now that was a trophy. A pair of tan slacks, way too big in the waist so he'd to double belt them. A sweat-shirt with the logo:

Clancy Brothers Live.

Yeah, how old was that?

Naturally, he'd gone through the guy's wallet. Twenty quid and a photo of a plain woman with three kids. He took both, found some lighter fuel and built a mound on the body, using clothes, newspapers and ten copies of *Goal*. Poured the fuel on the lot, said,

'You Kings of New England.'

He'd seen *Cider House Rules* on Sky Movies and the line had lodged. Most valuable of all, he found Cross's address book. Now, not only did he have a list of cops' homes, he even had a personal phone number for Brant. At the door, he tossed a match and moved fast.

I felt terribly tired, speed tired, like coming down from a crystal meth jag after a twenty-hour card game. The body still wants to run, nerved endings torqued to the pulsing tips of fingers and toes, but behind it, you start to shut down.

Tim Mc Loughlin
Heart of the Old Country

ROBERTS WAS TRYING to read the *Observer Magazine*, an article about 'Wagonistas'. It's sobriety but not the old-fashioned recovering addict, AA meetings stuff. This was being sober for a great lifestyle, for fashion, for economics. It was ten in the morning; Roberts lifted his mug, drank some of the red wine. He'd read once that it was good for the blood and heart. Though, if you drank it all day, maybe you were missing the point.

He was certainly missing his mouth.

A tremor caused the mug to hit the bridge of his nose and the stuff to spill down his front. He jumped up, trying to brush the liquid off. Wearing a pink dressing gown belonging to his wife, he hadn't shaved or washed in days, knew he was going down the toilet but couldn't summon up the energy to care. His daughter had been on a flying visit and borrowed fifty quid, then asked,

'Are you going to sell the house?'

'What house?'

She'd sighed eerily like her mother, then,

'This house. You can't live here, not with all Mummy's things.'

'And where will I go?'

'To a bedsit, like all solitary older men.'

He thought he'd misheard, repeated,

'Old... me?'

'Oh, Daddy, you were always old. Tariq says you should be retired.'

'You're still with him then?'

'Of course, he's my karma; we're going to Bombay to meet his family.'

Roberts felt a great weariness, said,

'Bon voyage.'

Now she near shrieked:

'We need money, we need you to sell up.'

Roberts counted to ten then tried,

'You tell Tariq to come and see me. We'll have a little chat.'

His daughter threw her eyes to heaven, then,

'Talk to you? Nobody can talk to you. Mummy said it was like talking to a brick wall.'

He didn't know how to proceed, so he said nothing. This riled her further. She spat:

'Oh, you're so pathetic, I hate you.'

And stormed out, slamming the door. He wanted to shout:

'Oh yeah? Give me back my fifty quid then.'

It crossed his mind to have Brant drop in on Tariq, expose him to that mind-set. Instead, he'd gone to the drinks cupboard and found nothing but bottles of red wine. He vaguely remembered going out the day after the funeral and buying another batch. Now he surveyed the empty bottles and thought he'd better shape up. Managed to stand under the shower and felt a degree better. Then he looked in the mirror and the shock made him gasp. An unshaven, red-eyed lunatic was staring back. That was it for any hope of shaving. He put on a crumpled suit, a grubby shirt and headed out, resolving to stock up on groceries, household goods, all that citizen shit. When he got to Safeway, the security guard eyed him closely. He hurried in, got a trolley and began to move down the aisle. He was lost. The shelves seemed stacked with huge amounts of washing powder. All he wanted was soup – as in one packet – some milk, bread and maybe a few slices of ham.

Heard someone whisper,

'Guv?'

Turned to face Falls. She was dressed in a white track-suit, emphasising her blackness. She looked in his empty trolley, asked,

'What are you doing?'

'Shopping.'

Falls pushed the trolley aside, asked,

'What do you need… everything?'

'Some red wine.'

'Oh, I don't think so. We need to get the essentials.'

He wanted to say,

'The wine is essential.'

But went with,

'I'll wait outside.'

He stood near the off-licence, wondering would he risk going for a bottle? A woman was passing, pulling a girl of eight or so by the hand. She stopped, rummaged in her bag, found some coins and shoved them at him, said in a testy tone,

'That's all the change I've got.'

And moved on, the little girl looking back, asking,

'Mum, is that a wino?'

'Sh... shu... shush, he'll hear you.'

He stared at the coins in his hand, shock sneaking along his spine. Falls appeared, pushing a heavy trolley, shouted,

'Give me a hand, eh?'

He put the coins in his pocket. Falls was driving a Daewoo, he asked,

'This yours?'

'Belongs to a neighbour, I do her shopping too.'

Opened the boot, began to put the stuff in, asked,

'You all right?'

'Never better.'

Back at his house, she surveyed the wreckage, asked,

'Have you been camping here?'

He sank into a chair, said,

'Give it a rest.'

She did.

He dozed, was awoken to the smell of cooking. The room was spotless. Falls handed him a mug, said,

'It's soup, you're frozen.'

To his surprise, it was good, awakened his appetite. She provided French bread, slices of meat and he ate it all, said,

'Christ, that was good.'

She gave a radiant smile. Lit up the whole room and he

realised with astonishment that he'd almost never seen her do that. He said,

'I think I'll be okay now.'

Falls stared at him for a long moment, considered, then:

'Yes, I think you just might.'

'I'm going to sell this house.'

'Great idea.'

'You think?'

'Yeah, who the fuck wants to live in Dulwich?'

'I thought everybody did.'

He was genuinely astonished. She gave another of the smiles, asked,

'How many black people do you know? I mean, as friends?'

'Ahm...'

'That's what I thought.'

She got all his soiled clothes in the washing machine, warned,

'Use fabric softener.'

'Why?'

'Jeez... men! Take it on trust, okay?'

She debated her next question, decided to risk it, went,

'I need a favour.'

He watched her face, gauged the intensity, asked,

'What?'

'A kid I know is in trouble. I need to get him off the hook.'

'Police trouble?'

'Yes.'

'How bad?'

'He and his mates gave a guy a good kicking.'

'And your interest is?'

Falls hung her head, her voice low, said,

'The skinhead, remember him?'

'Sure, he looked out for you when you went down the shitter.'

He paused, then exclaimed,

'Aw no, tell me you cut him loose, what? You thought you could change him? Jesus, Falls, it's him. He's the one did the kicking? Aw, for crying out loud.'

A silence between them, she had no defence, leastways none that would sound reasonable. Roberts gave a deep throat clearance, then:

'Okay, I'm not in any position to lecture you here. There's a DI, he'll know about it, he owes me from way back. His name is Nelson.'

'Thanks, sir, I really appreciate...'

Roberts' hand was up:

'Don't thank me yet, you haven't met Nelson. He's a piece of work; fact is, he makes Brant appear downright liberal.'

Get yourself a gay boyfriend! It's fantastic.
They're great cooks, they love shopping and
they're really frightened of you.

Jackie Clune

BRANT CHECKED HIS notebook:

Barry Weiss, with an address in New Cross.

Brant decided to head home, shower, then pay a visit to the guy. By the time he got to his flat, he felt his mind begin its shut down. Inside, he made some tea, tried to focus on what he was to do first. Oh yeah, shower. He sat in the armchair, put the tea on the floor for easy reach. The TV was directly in front, he stared at the blank screen. The tea went cold, he didn't move, just continued to stare at the screen.

Barry Weiss was in a phone kiosk, rang *The Tabloid*, got put through to the Dunphy, said,

'There's a fire at Sirinham Point. That's Meadow Road... but a match from the Oval Cricket Ground.'

'A fire?'

'And you'll want to know what your angle is?'

'Ahm... yes... please.'

'The second-floor flat, at the back, you'll find number three. You can count, right?'

'A third copper?'

'Gee, no wonder you're the crime capo. In case they start any nonsense about copycats, I used a new system.'

'Can you elaborate?'

'A hammer. Blunt enough for you? It was for him. I'll be eating brains for a week.'

Click.

Dunphy was rewinding the tape when the phone went again. He grabbed it, heard

'I thought of a name.'

'Name?'

'Is there an echo? Don't keep repeating everything, it's very annoying. "The Blitz", like Blitzkreig, know how to spell that?'

'Yes, but…'

'It's not negotiable.'

'The other papers…'

'Are shite, just do it.'

Click.

❒

The Tabloid led with:

BLITZ KILLS AGAIN

Exclusive Interview with serial police executioner

by

Top Crime Writer, Harold Dunphy

❒

Brant, if he'd turned on the telly, would have found it top story on every channel. He didn't. Continued to sit motionless, his mind a vacuum of white noise.

PORTER WAS UP to his arse in reporters, phones, leads, frustration. He shouted,

'Where the hell is Brant?'

No one had seen him. A tabloid guy named Dunphy, who had tapes of the killer, was demanding an interview. Porter had ignored him. It took three days for Brant to appear. When he did, his face had the look of a man who had been to hell and only part ways returned. Porter said,

'In the office. Now.'

Brant sat before the desk, his body language almost painful. Porter tried not to shout, went:

'Where have you been?'

'I'm not sure.'

'What?'

'I can't account for my movements. Isn't that the jargon?'

A thought hit Porter and he asked,

'You do know another policeman has been killed?'

Brant shook his head. Porter went to the door, grabbed a WPC, said,

'Give us some teas. Oh, and two Club Milks.'

She stared at him and he said,

'Did you hear me?'

'Sir, in view of the Sexual Discrimination Act, just because I'm female...'

'Get the fucking tea.'

She did.

Porter leant over Brant, said,

'A sergeant, name of Cross.'

An expression flitted across Brant's face. Porter would have been hard-pressed to label it. Was it shock, regret, pain? What it wasn't was anger. Porter would have preferred that. He continued:

'The killer is now calling himself "The Blitz". He used a hammer, then torched the flat. The Coroner says, despite the fire, they were able to do a full identification. Cross was not so much bludgeoned to death as beaten to pulp. They never saw such a beating in all their years. The killer has his own column in the papers.'

Brant finally moved, asked,

'How's that work?'

'He calls a hack named Dunphy, gives him the details.'

Porter indicated the cups, said,

'There's tea and... Club Milks.'

'I'm not doing tea. Dunphy, did you say?'

'Yes, you know him?'

'I do.'

Porter shuffled the avalanche of paper, asked,

'How did it go in New Cross?'

'New Cross? What's in New Cross?'

'Jesus, Brant. You were going to check out a likely lad, remember?'

Brant didn't answer and Porter added,

'Three days ago, you were to check on him.'

Brant was up, said,

'I'll go now.'

Porter stood, reaching for his jacket.

'I'm coming with you.'

As they hit the street, a man approached. He had the appearance of an accountant with his hand in the till, mid-thirties with his head shaved to a sheen, he said,

'Porter Nash!'

'What?'

'I'm Dunphy, from *The Tabloid*. I need to ask if you have anything?'

Before Porter could answer, Brant said,

'I've got something.'

Dunphy swivelled to face him, said,

'Yeah?'

Brant hit him in the gut and kept moving. As they got to the car, Porter asked,

'And what was that?'

'Didn't I say already? I knew him.'

❐

Barry was having a lie-in; he found fame more exhausting than he'd expected. The previous night he'd gone out and got steaming, really put them pints of lager away. Then a curry and collapsed into bed.

A pounding at his door. He shouted:

'Fuck off, I gave at the office.'

He was suffering – a headache from hell and his stomach doing a curried jig. More pounding, then:
    'Police.'

There is no such thing as a character curve.
There is a character and there is a curve. I don't
know where they join each other.
A guy starts the film hating blacks and by the
end, he's shagging a black girl; there's his charac-
ter curve. Well, thank you very much. Have I
really spent all my adult life learning that?

Smoking in Bed
Conversations with Bruce Robinson
Edited by Alistair Owen

FALLS DIDN'T KNOW how to dress to charm. She knew about intimidation, manipulation, but when you wanted a person to not only like you but to do you a favour, then what? She settled for her uniform. Roberts' contact, Nelson, was probably old school, she decided. Reminded herself to play the subservient card. When she'd finally got Nelson on the phone, he'd been gruff, said:

'What?'

'Chief Inspector Roberts suggested I talk to you, sir.'

'You're a woman?'

She wanted to shout:

'No wonder you're a detective.'

Kept her voice neutral, said,

'Yes, sir, a WPC.'

'Bloody nuisance.'

She didn't answer that, then he rasped,

'What do you want?'

She took a deep breath, said,

'A few nights back, an Arab got a bad beating.'

'Oh, that? Don't worry, we got two of the scumbags. The third one we havn't found yet but we know who he is.'

Looking down at her hands, she realised her fingers were crossed, said,

'He's the one I want to discuss.'

Silence as he weighed the numbers, she continued:

'Could I buy you breakfast?'

'I can always use a breakfast.'

'Great... in an hour?'

'Two hours. There's a café called Romero's, know it?'

'Yes.'

She didn't.

Click.

There's a level below transport café – not a level you'd want to reach. Construction workers will warn you away from them, that's a warning you better heed. Known to cab drivers as 'dives', you literally dive in and out, coffee being the only item related to a taste zone. Romero's was a dive. It took Falls the two hours to find it. Being in uniform didn't help. An OAP asked,

'Going to shut it down? Not before bloody time.'

And a young woman who said,

'Oh, you don't want to go there, it's ghastly.'

It was.

If the windows had ever been cleaned, no one remembered. A grubby sign proclaimed:

'Tuesday's special, Toad-in-the-hole.'

She went in. Dim fluorescent light bathed the interior in suicidal yellow. All the tables save one were empty. Falls had projected Nelson as a Brant clone: big, thick, ugly. A man in a tweed jacket was sitting at the furthest table. In his mid-thirties, he had a mop of thick brown hair, a face that BBC newsreaders would describe as craggy and a solid build. He smiled and she felt a stir. The kind of smile that bathes you in its welcome, made you feel its delight was solely at the sight of you. He said,

'Falls?'

'Yes, sir.'

'Are you going to guard the door or come and sit down?'

Why the hell hadn't Roberts told her the guy was a hunk? Now that she thought about it, he'd had a sly smile as he told her. Totally thrown, she moved and took a chair. Up close, Nelson was even better. Brown wide eyes, ah... yes. She was a sucker for those. Pulled her mind to a halt, chided herself: So what? Roberts implied this guy was a bigot and that wiped out any physical attraction... right, course it did.

Then realised he was speaking, heard:

'Falls, hello, you in there?'

'Sorry. With the killings, we're all a bit strung out.'

He smiled and she felt the pang as he asked,

'What will you have? I strongly advise you to avoid the toad-in-the-hole.'

'Tea. Tea, sir.'

Shook his head.

'Enough with the "sir", I'm Bob.'

And held out his hand. Long tapered fingers and – wonders – clean nails, cuticles pushed back, hands that were cared for. She immediately checked for a ring, nope, no ring. His grasp was strong and she wanted to shout,

'To hell with foreplay, let's do it.'

The proprietor emerged from the shadows, looking but a drink from the street. Nelson said,

'Tea and toast for two.'

She adored that 'two'. Turning back to her, he said,

'You can smoke if you want.'

'I don't smoke, sir... Bob.'

He laughed, repeated,

'Sir Bob! Mind you, if you did smoke, it could only help in here, maybe kill off the bacteria. To tell the truth, though, I don't like women who smoke.'

She wanted to shout:

'Me neither.'

But bit down. He reached in his pocket, took out a notebook, began,

'Okay, we've got two of the guys involved in the assault.'

She grasped at the word:

'Assault? He's not...?'

'Dead? No, God knows how, they did a real number on him. When those skins start in with the steel-cap boots, it's serious. The two we nabbed are singing like canaries, gave up the third guy without a second thought and he's – let me see, I can hardly read my own writing – John Wales, known as "Metal". This is the guy you wanted to discuss?'

'Yes.'

'What is he, a snitch?'

She couldn't believe it: here was an explanation, a plausible one. Nodding furiously, she said,

'If there's any way you can cut him loose?'

Nelson put the notebook away, leant back in his chair, said,

'Anything can be buried.'

'Will you?'

'Will I? What's it worth?'

Falls sighed. Frigging cops, it always came down to barter, she answered:

'A lot.'

'Come for a drink tomorrow night.'

'That's all?'

Now she got that smile but it seemed to have lost some of its wattage, he said,

'You've been around, you know it's never "That's all".'

'Okay.'

'I'll pick you up around eight.'

'That's fine, let me give you my address.'

'I have it.'

'You know where I live?'

'Jeez, Falls, what a stupid question.'

Well, no one would ever accuse Frank of being too human. One thing was certain though, there wasn't anyone else you'd want to be riding with when the death house was calling your name.

George P Pelecanos
Shame the Devil

BARRY PULLED ON a sweatshirt, track bottoms, opened the door. He recognised Brant but didn't register the fact. Porter asked,

'Mr Weiss, Barry Weiss?'

'That's me.'

'Might we step in?'

And flashed their warrant cards. Barry decided to bust their balls, asked,

'Got a warrant?'

Brant gave a tiny smile, pushed Barry in the chest, followed him in, said,

'It's in the post.'

Barry could see the other cop wasn't happy with the Gestapo tactics so he'd work on him. Without a further word, Brant began a search. Barry looked at Porter, asked,

'Get you anything? Coffee, nice drop of absinthe?'

'Drop of what?'

'Yeah, I won it. You want to get this month's *Bizarre*, got my letter in there, won the prize.'

'You write a lot of letters, Mr Weiss?'

Barry gave a resigned shrug, said,

'Who's got the time?'

Brant was back, said,

'Nothing.'

Barry kept his eyes on Porter, asked,

'What were you looking for, maybe I can help you?'

Brant caught him by the collar of his sweatshirt, pulled him into the chair, said,

'You're a real helpful guy.'

Porter moved over, asked,

'What do you do, Mr Weiss?'

'I'm between jobs.'

'You like to beat up on people?'

'What?'

'At the gym, you clobbered a guy pretty good.'

'Oh, that. Bloody fruit came on to me, I gave him a clip.'

He caught the look between the cops, quickly added,

'Not that I've anything against homosexuals.'

Brant asked,

'And policemen, how do you feel about them?'

'Thank God, I say, thank God for the men in blue.'

Barry could feel the aggression from Brant, knew how badly the cop wanted to lash out. But the other guy, the fag, he was a restraining influence. Then something clicked in Brant's eyes and he asked,

'Do I know you?'

'If we'd met, I'm sure I'd remember.'

Porter said,

'Let's go.'

At the door, Brant said,

'You're dirty, Barry. Of what I don't know, but I'll be keeping an eye on you.'

After they'd gone, Barry said:

'Fucking amateurs.'

Outside, Porter asked,

'What do you think?'

'He's a bad one but if he's the one, I don't know.'

They stood for a moment, then Brant said:

'You're thinking, if he is our guy, in the past three days he butchered Cross. If I'd gone to check him out, earlier…'

'That's pure speculation.'

'Not for Cross it isn't.'

Trailing that shadow, they went into a pub. Porter said,

'I'm buying.'

'Good, a pint and a chaser.'

The barman, recognising the heat, said,

'On me, gents.'

Porter pushed the money across, asked,

'Did I indicate we were free-loading?'

'No… but.'

'Then get my change.'

When they'd moved to a table, the barman muttered,

'Like I'm supposed to be fucking impressed.'

Brant gulped his pint, belched, said,

'Admirable as that was, you've only confused the poor bastard.'

'I don't do bribes.'

'Leastways not yet.'

'What's that mean?'

'That you've a lot to learn, give it time.'

When they got back to the station, Porter noticed the

amused looks from the other cops, checked with the desk
sergeant who said,

'You better take a peek at the notice board.'

A large black-and-white photo of Brant and Porter,
almost joined, was pinned there. A bold caption read:

Hands-on policing.
(Renfrew Road, home to Porter Nash)

Brant gave a thin smile, said,
'Good likeness.'
Porter tore it down, swore,
'Bloody morons.'

❏

Barry Weiss was reflecting on the visit from the cops. The
fascist one, Brant, would certainly call again. Barry
couldn't operate with the threat of that over him. He
dressed in black levis, black T-shirt and the bomber jacket,
headed out. Caught a bus that brought him right outside
Waterloo Station. He headed upstairs to the main concourse, was happy to see the crowds of people. Moving at
a brisk pace, he found the lockers and opened his. A smile
lit his face as he surveyed the trophies. What the cops
wouldn't give to find these. He selected Cross's wallet and
address book, shut the locker, went to a designer coffee
outlet. The assistant, a girl in her twenties, smiled and he
said,

'Tall latte.'

Pulled out the wallet and saw the girl's eyes glance at the photo, the woman and three kids. He said,

'My family.'

'Lovely.'

As she handed across the coffee, he added,

'All killed in a car accident.'

'Oh my God.'

He sat in her line of vision, revelling in her shock. Opened the address book and began to flick through, mouthing, 'Eeny, meeney miney, mo.' The end coincided with Falls. He looked at her address, said,

'Tonight, my sweet.'

Every romance that takes itself seriously must have a warp of fear and horror.

JRR Tolkien

FALLS TRIED TO sort through her feelings. Sure, she was attracted to Nelson, no argument there. The guy had most of the moves and wasn't afraid to use them. But, he'd coerced her into the date. The stupid bastard, she'd have gone willingly. She glanced at the clock: he was due in twenty minutes, time for some Jack. She poured a small measure, considered then poured again. What would Rosie have said?

'Go for it, gal; use him up, throw him away.'

Yeah.

She'd dressed, not so much down as with indifference. A white T, extra large that hid her shape, black Farrah slacks and flat black heels. No sex in that arena. The Jack gave her a jolt and she moved up a level, feeling mellow. Had heard a young boy shout at his mother in the supermarket:

'Mom, take a chill pill.'

That's what she was doing, chilling out and it felt fine. As she smoothed the line on her pants, she remembered PC Tone. A fresh-faced newcomer, he'd tried to impress Brant. Went after a ruthless pair of Irish villains who'd killed him for his pants.

Crease that.

The same pair had very nearly taken Brant down too. She knew he felt responsible for the young cop's death and odd times went to the grave. But would he ever talk about it, open up? Would he fuck. She'd washed her hair with L'Oréal something-or-other and it looked good. On the commercials, all those white chicks purring:

'Because I'm worth it.'

She hated them. All that girly simpering shit, made her want to scream. Her drink was gone. How did that happen? The radio was tuned to a local Brixton station and here was Mary J Blige with 'Family Affair'. Falls sang along, moved to the sofa and put on her black denim jacket, turned the collar up, checked herself in the mirror, said,

'All—right!'

She'd put fresh sheets on the bed, in case... in case the night got away from her. The doorbell went. Before she opened, she checked through the peephole then, reassured, she turned the lock.

He had dressed up: dark navy suit, white shirt and tie, police shoes. Looking good, he held out chocolates and flowers, said,

'I don't know if people do this any more.'

'They should, come in.'

He did a cop scan of the room, checking where the exits were. She asked,

'Like a drink?'

'Sure, give you time to get ready.'

'I am ready.'

'Oh… right.'

Poured him some Jack and a small one for herself, went,

'Cheers.'

'Yeah.'

He was off balance, his composure rattled, so she relented, said,

'I can still change.'

'No, you're fine.'

When a man uses 'fine' to a woman, it's like saying you've nice eyes, meaning you're a dog but I'd better throw you something. He knocked back the drink and asked,

'Ready?'

'As ever.'

He was driving a Rover, impressed her by opening the door for her, then moved round to let himself in. As he put the car in gear, he asked:

'Italian okay?'

'Sure.'

'I booked a place at the Elephant, it's got a rep.'

'But for what?'

And they both lightened up. The evening went well from there. They'd two bottles of wine with the food and he was well able to talk. Most cops, it's shop talk and the job and… the job. He never mentioned their work, spoke about music, movies, travel. When the coffee came, he said,

'You haven't said a whole lot.'

'I like listening to you.'

He gave her a full look, asked,

'So, we might do it again?'

'I'd say so.'

On the drive back to her place, she was anticipating him spending the night, the prospect sent a shiver through her. After he parked the car, he leant over and she closed her eyes in anticipation of the kiss.

Nothing happened.

He was unlocking her door, saying,

'I had a really nice time, I'll call you.'

She couldn't believe it. Clean sheets, wild anticipation and he'd "Call her!"

She asked,

'When?'

'When what?'

'When will you call me? Later to see if I'm safely tucked in? Tomorrow, next week... some bright day in August?'

'Jeez, Falls. I...'

'Look, Nelson, I'm too tired for games. A man says "I'll call" and the woman begins the countdown, waiting and hoping. He thinks, tomorrow or Sunday, what's the difference? Let me tell you, there's a hell of a bloody difference.'

She began to get out, he said,

'Tomorrow. I'll call you tomorrow.'

'Piss off.'

And slammed the door. He stared at her through the windscreen then put the car in gear, moved away. She wanted to call him back, muttered,

'Dumb, dumb, dumb... shit.'

Began to rummage in her purse. Where were those

bloody keys? Barry Weiss moved out of the shadows, hammer raised.

I was lighting us both a cigarette when he turned
to me and said, 'Sorry if I got cross, Morrie.'
'That's all right,' I said.
'Bit of an edge, I suppose.'
It was all very kosher and British.
'Not surprising' I said. 'It's been an angstful sort
of night.'

Derek Raymond
The Crust On Its Uppers

THE SUPER WAS not pleased to see Roberts, especially as he was having his tea break. A daily ritual, he had two cups and two rich tea biscuits. What he liked to do was clear his desk, dunk the biscuits and slow dribble them into his mouth. Damn close to being the highlight of his day. He was mid-ribble when Roberts walked in. The Super, his head back, mouth wide – like Homer Simpson – was not a picture of leadership or authority. He near choked on being caught, went:

'I didn't hear you knock.'

Roberts launched:

'You replaced me.'

'What?'

'Porter Nash is heading up the inquiry.'

'You're on compassionate leave.'

'I'm back.'

The Super looked longingly at the tea, resolved to get Roberts out fast, asked,

'How do you feel about early retirement?'

Roberts smiled bleakly, answered,

'We'd miss you, sir.'

The Super told himself he was dealing with a lunatic. Hazel, the police shrink, had once told him that grief unhinges the mind. Here was the proof that Hazel knew his stuff, and who'd ever have thought he was a dipsomaniac? It was still a shock to realise that his own puppet McDonald had shafted him. He'd have to re-evaluate that young man. Now he straightened his back, tried for resolve, which he hoped he was famous for, said,

'There are other urgent cases.'

'I'll take them.'

Surprised he hadn't gotten an argument, the Super said in a reconciliatory tone,

'Losing a wife isn't easy.'

Roberts' face lit up, he asked,

'You lost your wife, sir?'

'Well, no... I...'

'Then, with all due respect, sir, how the hell would you know what it's like?'

And then he was gone. Didn't even wait to be dismissed. Skin had formed over the tea and the Super splashed the biscuit into it, said,

'A lunatic, that's for sure.'

❐

Roberts went through the current cases. Christ, it was depressing. If it was war on the streets, the police had already lost. He flicked through accounts of rape, fraud, arson, burglary and considered going home. Let the tide of anarchy wash over them. Shook himself and selected a file at random.

Okay.

Pensioners were being targeted in their homes. An intruder broke in during the night, beat the occupant mercilessly and stole whatever money he could. The only description was that the assailant was white and in his twenties. Roberts put the file down, he saw McDonald cruise by, called to him, said,

'Get me a map of Southwark.'

'Now?'

'Next Sunday? Course it's now and be quick about it.'

He was.

Roberts looked up the addresses of those attacked and studied the pattern. McDonald, leaning over his shoulder, offered,

'That's a dead-end case, sir. I did the door-to-door myself, nothing came of it.'

Roberts took out his pen, made some marks on the map, said,

'See those marks?'

'Yes, sir.'

'Those are the buildings where the pensioners live.'

'Right, sir.'

'Now, see how they almost circle this building here.'

'I see that, sir, but…'

'Shut up. Any guess as to what that building is?'

'Not offhand, sir.'

Roberts pushed back from the map, looked at McDonald, asked,

'Ever wonder why you're still a constable?'

'Well, sir, I…'

'Because you're a sloppy bastard. You do the minimum and away home with you. Jeez, a traffic warden has more balls. That building is the main post office and what happens there, do you think?'

McDonald wanted to shrug and say,

'Not a whole lot.'

But thought harder, then:

'Pensions.'

'Brilliant. So what you do is go there on the next pay-out day, watch for a white male in his twenties who's loitering and then you get back to me.'

'Yes, sir.'

'Okay, let's see if we can solve another.'

Along the Walworth Road, people were being mugged for their mobile phones. Thing was, if the phones weren't new, the mugger flung them back. Roberts said,

'That's not a crime, that's a public service.'

Roberts couldn't believe it, he was enjoying himself, the andrenalin rush was pure bliss. He said,

'See McDonald, if you'd solved those two, you'd be on your way to sergeant.'

McDonald had never liked Roberts, now he hated him. Decided to brown-nose, maybe the superior prick would kick the credit for those cases his way. Said,

'It's a learning experience to watch a professional at work.'

Roberts let out a sigh, then:

'I never actually believed people spoke like that. You certainly can't have picked it up in Glasgow. What, you watch The Oprah Show, pick up a few pointers? Well, son, that might cut some ice with the Super but it don't mean shit to me. Now, piss off and check out the post office.'

He opened another file. Young boys were being attacked on Clapham Common, usually on the way home from school. He made a note to arrange for a daily police patrol when the schools let out. It wouldn't stop the attacks but it would definitely interrupt them. Standing up, he stretched, cast an eye on the pile of cases waiting, said,

'At least I've dented them.'

Headed for the canteen. McDonald was there, wolfing a bacon sandwich. Roberts said,

'Didn't I tell you to go somewhere?'

'Well yes, but I thought a bit of sustenance first.'

'You thought wrong, get moving.'

McDonald began to pack away the food and Roberts barked:

'Leave it.'

After the PC had skulked off, Roberts sat, realised he was hungry, checked the contents, Yeah, ketchup on double bacon slice and a hint of tomato. He took a healthy bite.

He said, 'You get some bad news?'
She didn't answer. Just kept looking like she was
in some kind of state.
He said 'Well' and moved to the door. It was as
he reached it, about to go out, he heard her say,
'You followed him, didn't you?'
Elvin kept going. There was no talking to an
upset, emotional woman.

Elmore Leonard
Maximum Bob

BARRY WEISS HAD put all his weight behind the swing of the hammer. He wanted to nail this in one, heard a roar and a figure came hurtling at him, hitting him full-on. Barry went over, the figure on top of him. The woman was screaming. Barry managed to roll, came up in a crouch. The figure was a skinhead and as Barry registered this, he swung the hammer, connecting with the forehead, then he was up and running for all he was worth.

Falls wished the screaming would stop then realised it was her. Put a hand to her mouth and then slowly approached the figure on the ground. It was Metal. She tried for a pulse, couldn't find one and heard the screaming again.

❏

Porter and Brant were in Falls' living room. A doctor had given her a sedative and she was sleeping. Brant found the bottle of Jack, poured one, offered it to Porter who shook his head, asked,

'Should we be taking her booze?'

'She won't be counting.'

Brant knocked the drink back, grimaced then said,

'I hate this shit.'

Porter didn't know if he meant the situation or the drink, was too het up to care, said,

'The skinhead's dead?'

'As a doornail.'

Brant shrugged and Porter asked,

'She get a look at her attacker?

'Only that he was white, said all white guys look the same to her.'

Porter felt powerless. He wanted to lash out, do something, asked,

'She know the skinhead is dead?'

'Yes, she knows.'

'What's the deal here? I mean, a black woman, a black policewoman and what... a skinhead guardian angel?'

Brant gave his smile, said,

'Welcome to the liberal south-east, and you thought we were rednecks.'

Nelson arrived, strode up to them, near shouted,

'Is she all right?'

Porter looked at Brant who said nothing, then back to Nelson.

'What are you, a boyfriend?'

Nelson produced his warrant card, said,

'I'm on the Job.'

Brant sniggered and Nelson gave him the stare, then:

'I heard someone got killed.'

'Falls is okay. Our cop killer took a run at her and some skinhead tried to save her, got his ticket punched.'

Nelson took a deep breath, then:

'Metal... John something or other, runner with the British National Party.'

Porter's interest was up, asked,

'You had dealings with him?'

'No, I knew of him, through another case.'

Porter studied Nelson, then:

'Were you with her this evening?'

'Yes, I dropped her off.'

'You didn't think to walk her to her door?'

'I...'

Brant joined, said,

'What a gent.'

Then turned his back, said to Porter,

'I'll sit with her.'

'You sure?'

''Course.'

Nelson wanted to volunteer but he'd effectively been frozen out. He turned and left without another word.

❏

Barry Weiss was rattled. He'd run till his lungs burst, convinced the cops were going to grab him at any moment. He leant against a wall to get his bearings, knew he had to get off the street. Across the road was a pub and he headed over. A siren sounded and it sounded near. Barry walked up to the bar and a barmaid gave him a curious look, said,

'You running a marathon?'

He felt the hammer's weight in his pocket, wanted to grab it, give her a lash across the face, say,

'Run that.'

He wiped the sweat from his brow, said,

'Two pints of lager.'

Got those and moved to a table. His heart was palpitating, a tremor in his hands. He sunk the first pint in one long, desperate gulp, thought: That's the business.

In a few minutes, he felt the panic ease, thought: Jeez, that was close. If the woman had joined in, helped instead of screaming, I would have been in deep shit.

He knew he'd fucked up, should have gone after her once the skinhead was out of the picture. As he began the second pint, he tried to recall if Bundy or Gacy had fucked up. Sure they had, victims escaping from both of them. And... They got caught, how much more could you fuck up? He was still free but he'd have to be careful. When closing time came, he left with the crowd of people who'd drawn out last orders. The pints had restored him and he could feel his adrenalin sing. On the street, there was no sign of cops and Barry decided to restore his confidence. As the crowd began to disperse, hailing cabs, moving to the underground, he had to make a rapid choice. A man in an expensive leather jacket was waving goodbye. Barry fell in behind him, the man's friends calling:

'John, John, sure you don't want to come to the club?'

'No, I've an early start.'

Barry wanted to add,

'Earlier than you think, mate.'

The man turned left, walked unsteadily and Barry caught up, said,

'John.'

John turned and Barry moved in close, saying,

'Jeez, John. What's your hurry?'

Kneed him in the balls, caught him as he fell, got him to a doorway, took a look around. No one paying any attention, Barry went through his pockets, saying,

'If you'd gone to the club, you'd have got really hammered.'

Took his wallet, loose change and heard people coming along, he stepped away, moved quickly up the street, thinking, A curry, I could really murder one.

❐

The local police put John's attack down to the usual mugging. He protested,

'He took my wallet, my wages were in there.'

'Hey, you could have been killed.'

'Sure, like that was ever going to happen.'

I'm just admitting that there are such things for us to think about in this day and age when a man can't wear a hat anymore on the street.

Sam Kashner
Sinatraland

McDONALD PLANNED TO solve the attacks on the pensioners. Roberts had told him to case the post office and report back. He said, 'Will I? Will I fuck.' This was his time to shine, get noticed and back into the Super's good books. He'd not mention Roberts at all. Let the whole glorious event be his. Waking early, he felt ready, his mind alert. Wore casual clothes and, at the post office, asked for the boss, showed him his warrant card, outlined the plan. The guy was all cooperation, showed him a counter from which he could see everything without being seen.

Perfect.

Meant he could sit if it proved to be a long day. It did. After four hours, he was bored rigid. The staff kept him supplied with tea and now he badly needed to pee. Then thought: Hello, you again.

Twice a guy in his twenties had passed him, an hour apart. The guy was so ordinary, he almost hadn't registered: dressed in a parka, thick black-rimmed glasses and lank long hair. You looked at him, your eyes kept moving as your mind said 'geek', 'nerd' and searched for something more interesting. McDonald locked on him. The guy had a furtive, shifty look. Then he turned, headed for the door. McDonald went after him. The boss, sensing drama, asked,

'You see something?'

But got no reply.

Outside, McDonald couldn't see the geek, thought he'd lost him. Rage and frustration tore through his mind. Then, in the small café across the road, he spotted him, ordering takeaway chips. When he came out, McDonald positioned himself to follow. The geek walked towards Lee Road, took a right and entered a building. McDonald was close behind, saw the geek go up the first flight of stairs and was almost on top of him as he searched for his keys. McDonald said,

'This your place?'

'Who are you?'

'The police. I asked you a question?'

'Yes, yes it is. Is something wrong?'

'Let's take it inside.'

The geek opened the door and McDonald pushed him in. The chips fell and McDonald felt them squish beneath his boots. He slammed the door and moved after the geek, glanced round the flat. To his surprise it was neat, with books tidily arranged, newspapers and magazines stacked on a small table. He asked,

'What are you, a student?'

'Ahm, yes, accountancy. Look, I don't know what you want...'

McDonald had seen Brant in action, heard the stories told with awe and admiration. What Brant did was ignore all the rules and get away with it. McDonald was tired of toeing the line and getting nowhere. He was going to have some of that maverick magic. He was nose to nose with the geek and head-butted him. The glasses and nose broke in unison. McDonald then gut-punched him and walked over to the window, opened it wide. He couldn't believe the rush, the sheer power he felt. Indicating the window, he said,

'You're going out that if I don't get the answers I want.'

The geek was crying now, on his knees, sniffed,

'Tell me what you want. I haven't done anything.'

McDonald stood over him, went,

'You're crying. Were the old folk crying when you attacked them, eh?'

'What?'

He began to stand up, blood pouring from his nose. McDonald was about to berate further when the geek lunged, he had hold of McDonald's shirt and they fell back against the window. McDonald tried to break the grip, hit out with his left fist, the geek staggered, tried to get his balance and fell out the window. McDonald was stunned, heard the thump and took a quick look. The geek had landed in a utility yard, his neck turned at an impossible angle. McDonald said,

'Oh fuck.'

For a moment, he was lost, then jerked into motion. Out the door, down the stairs and on to the street, he knew he should call an ambulance but tried to reason with himself:

'No, no, it's too late.'

Passing a pub, he wanted to go in, hammer down a line

of whiskies. But he might never stop. His heart was pounding, fright coursing through his system.

❐

Brant arrived at the station looking like he'd been up all night, which he had. Porter said,

'Jeez, you look rough.'

'I feel it.'

'How is Falls?'

'She's up, moving around but in that zone of delayed shock.'

Porter was swamped with reports, files, said,

'I don't suppose she feels it but she was lucky. If not for the skinhead, she'd be another statistic.'

Brant got out his Weights, cranked the Zippo and was soon engulfed by smoke. Porter sat, seemed to weigh something, then,

'How do you feel about weddings?'

'Weddings? Jeez, I give them a wide berth. Why, you thinking of taking the plunge?'

'Not me, my father.'

'You're kidding, you mean you'll be legitimate then?'

'I'm serious, he's 65 and he's going to marry his secretary who's, like… thirty.'

'And you want me to go?'

'I'd have asked Falls but under the circumstances… I don't want to turn up on my own.'

Brant ground out the cig on the floor, gave a tight smile, said,

'Sure, long as they don't have me down as your… signif-
icant other.'

Porter lightened, said,

'They don't think much of me but I don't think even
they would see me as that desperate.'

Brant stood.

'Don't knock it, boyo. Couple of drinks and I improve
out of all recognition.'

'Christ, it would take an awful lot of drink. It's
Saturday, at The Carmelite Church on Kensington Church
Street.'

Brant turned to face him, asked,

'Catholic? I's a catholic gig?'

'So, you have a problem there?'

'No, but there's always a shitload of guilt in the air. Add
booze and watch out.'

'That's why I'm taking you.'

'For the aggro?'

'No, the guilt.'

1983
It was a beautiful day. Walked on the street and
a little kid, she was six or seven, with another
kid, yelled, 'Look at the guy with the wig' and I
was really embarrassed, I blew my cool and it
ruined my afternoon. So I was depressed.

Andy Warhol

ROBERTS HAD CLEARED three more cases. One was a hit and run, which he solved by going round to see the family of the victim. Turned out a brother had been the driver and had been nursing an imagined slight for years. As soon as Roberts began talking to him, he confessed, which was police work at its most basic – talking to those involved. Next, a purse-snatcher operating in Kennington Park. A snitch had given up the perp in five minutes flat. The third was a stolen-car operation out of Streatham. Again, simple procedure had solved the case. Roberts placed surveillance on dodgy garages in the area and caught the gang red-handed. Admittedly, these were not the brightest of villains but their apprehension appeared greater than it was.

The station was buzzing with his triumph, cops had been congratulating him at every opportunity. His success made them all look good. The Super was astounded, sent for Roberts and got the bottle out of the drawer. Roberts said,

'No thanks, sir; not while I'm on duty.'

The bottle went back in the desk.

'By jove, Roberts, you've done a commendable body of work there.'

Roberts put it down to luck and having no home life. What else was there to do? The cases kept him from brooding. He said,

'Thank you, sir.'

'I believe you've been putting in Trojan hours of extra hours.'

'I felt it was necessary, sir.'

'And you were right. By God, you're an example to us all. I thought after your wife died, well, I thought you were finished.'

'Your faith kept me going, sir.'

The Super examined Roberts' face for a sign of impertinence, didn't see any and continued:

'Pity Porter Nash and his team won't take a leaf out of your book. I can't promise anything but it's very likely you'll be replacing him. As acting inspector, he has proved sadly inadequate. Those people – queers – they don't have the staying power.'

Roberts had no answer to the blatant homophobia and didn't attempt one. The Super straightened his back, said,

'You're somewhat close to Falls?'

'Close, sir?'

'As well as being her superior officer, you two have a friendship, I mean, you can talk to her?'

'Yes sir, I can talk to her.'

The Super sighed.

'Yer darkies, I never fully trust them; they hate us, you know.'

'Do they, sir?'

'By God they do, resent us for being on top. Don't you ever forget you're a white man, Chief Inspector.'

Roberts considered the many insane replies available but instead just nodded. It seemed to be what the Super expected, he continued:

'Good man. When they come rioting down the Brixton Road – and they will, mark my words – you'll do well to know on which side of the barricade you belong.'

Roberts was seriously regretting his refusal of the drink. Much more of this and he'd lunge for the bottle, but the tirade was winding down, the Super lowered his voice.

'You'll know she had some connection to the Nazi who got killed?'

'Ahm, I heard he saved her life.'

The Super waved a hand in scornful dismissal.

'She intends going to the funeral, can you imagine?'

'Well, sir, they were friends.'

'Balls, friends! A Nazi and a nigger. Weren't you paying attention before?'

'Yes sir, I hung on every word and believe me, I won't forget it ever.'

'See you don't. Now, the Hitler boys will be out in force, a fallen comrade and all that rubbish, so you're to keep her from going.'

'Stop her?'

'Use your charm, man. I'm told you used to have buckets of it. Failing that, threaten her. Don't forget, you'll be heading up the murder inquiry soon, you'll need mettle for that. Here's a chance to get some practice.'

Ken Bruen

'Is that all, sir?'
'Yes, tell my secretary I'm ready for my tea.'
Outside, Roberts took a deep breath. Brant approached, said,
'I hear you'll be heading the inquiry.'
'Maybe. Meantime I have to talk to Falls.'
'Good luck.'
'Want to tag along? Be like old times.'
'Can't, I'm going to a wedding.'
'Oh, anyone I know?'
Brant looked him full in the face, smiled, said,
'I very much doubt it.'
Roberts forgot to tell the secretary about the tea.

❏

Outside Falls' place, a Rover was parked. Roberts clocked it straightaway, tapped on the window, said,
'Nelson.'
He opened the door and got in. The car reeked of booze and curry. Nelson looked rough, red-eyed and unshaven. Roberts, not long from the same situation, asked,
'What's this, a stakeout?'
'Sort of. I'm keeping an eye on who calls.'
Nelson's voice was ragged, a hoarseness as if he'd been shouting all night. Roberts realised the man was seriously wired, said,
'Does she know you're here?'
'Yes, but she won't talk to me.'
'Give her some time, she's had a close call.'

Nelson turned to Roberts, his eyes fucked, said,

'But I screwed up, literally delivered her to the killer.'

'What?'

'You don't know? We'd been out and I drove her back here, didn't even get out of the car, just let her go and I drove off. The guy waiting there with a hammer.'

Roberts didn't think platitudes would help so he went with:

'You fucked up.'

'Big time.'

'We all do, she'll get over it.'

'You think?'

'I don't know.'

He started to get out and Nelson asked,

'Will you put a word in for me?'

'Sure.'

See
no matter what you have done
I am still here
And it has made me dangerous and wise
And brother
You cannot whore, perfume and
Suppress me any more
I have my own business in this skin
And on this planet.

Gail Murray

ROBERTS FOUND HIMSELF anxious as he rang Falls'
bell. He expected to find her in a terrible state and wasn't
sure he had what it took to haul her back. No answer. A
guilty relief began to sweep over him, but then the door
opened. Falls was dressed in a spotless white sweatshirt
with dark navy jeans. Her feet were bare, giving her an air
of relaxation. She said,

'Oh.'

He couldn't think of a single form of greeting and stood
there like an idiot. She glanced over his shoulder at Nelson
sitting in the car, grimaced and said,

'Come in.'

The place was neat, tidy and smelling of airfreshener.
She indicated a chair and as he sat, she said,

'Tea?'

'Great.'

She arrived back with a tray holding teapot, cups, biscuits. While she poured, Roberts took a good look at her
and had to admit she was looking good, no, looking great.
Catching his scrutiny, she went:

'What?'

'I was thinking how well you seem.'

Anger in her eyes, she snapped,

'You expected what? Tears? Hysteria? Let me tell you, I'm all through with that grieving shit. After Rosie, I went to pieces. You want to know something? I'm glad that maniac didn't kill me. But let me guess, they sent you to talk me out of the funeral? Don't waste your time, I'm going.'

He sipped his tea, said,

'Okay.'

Took her by surprise and she asked,

'That's it, you're not going to argue?'

'Nope.'

'Oh.'

He let her digest that, until,

'You might give Nelson a break.'

'Fuck him.'

'Did he help you out, when you went to him?'

'Yeah.'

'Then cut the crap, he's a cop, get off your high horse.'

She eyeballed him, assessing how far he could be pushed, figured she'd had her limit, said,

'I'll think about it.'

'Think all you want, I want him at the funeral with you.'

Then he stood, said,

'You need to talk, you know where I am.'

'Thanks, I think.'

He reached out, touched her shoulder. The gesture took them both by surprise. He said,

'The hard-ass act, it works for Brant. Anyone else, it wipes out.'

For a moment her eyes clouded, then she got a grip, said,

'It's getting me through, isn't that the point?'

Roberts considered, said,

'I have no idea what the point is or even if there ever was one but I do know you can't hack it alone.'

'You seem to.'

'And what did it get me? You found me wandering the supermarket like a wino. No, that maverick shit is over-rated.'

❏

Porter Nash had another frustrating day. A ton of leads had been followed up but nothing came of them. The Press were screaming about police incompetence and a prime time TV programme had lashed their failure. An atmosphere of depression had settled on the station. As Porter called it a day and headed out, not even the desk sergeant said goodnight. Bad sign. The desk was a thermometer of the force. No matter how bad things got, the duty sergeant would usually find a cliché to rally the troops. Not today. Brant was leaning against his car, smoking, asked,

'Want to come for a brewski?'

'Sure, why not?'

Brant drove, heading towards the Oval. His driving was a model of controlled ferocity. Porter asked,

'Where are we headed?'

'Lorn Road. Think forlorn.'

'There's a pub there?

'Fuck no, it's residential. I live there.'

'We're going to your place?'

Brant glanced at him, grinned, said,

'Yeah, and don't get any ideas.'

'I'm surprised is all.'

'I don't get too many visitors, so excuse the mess. I figure, you let me in your gaff, I'll return the compliment. You hungry? Want fish and chips?'

'No thanks.'

As they parked, Porter swept his eyes across the street. Nothing untoward was happening. It was one of those rare pockets of quiet in the maelstrom that was the Oval. He asked,

'How'd you wash up here?'

'I leaned on a landlord, leaned hard.'

When they got to the front door, Porter looked back at the car, asked,

'Is it safe there?'

And got the wolf smile with,

'Mine is.'

The living room was crammed with books. Centrepiece was a large photo of what appeared to be some kind of docks. Brant said,

'That's the Claddagh in Galway. You know, where the rings originated?'

Porter stepped closer, could make out swans on the water, said,

'Must be a peaceful place.'

Brant snorted, said,

'Last time I was there, some nutter was beheading swans. There are no peaceful places, not any more. You want peace, carry a piece. Sit down.'

Brant disappeared into the kitchen, returned with a tray, a bottle of what appeared to be water and two heavy tumblers. He set them down, said,

'That's poteen, Irish moonshine.'

'Isn't it illegal?'

'I fucking hope so.'

He poured substantial measures, said,

'*Slàinte.*'

'Okay.'

Porter was expecting a lethal kick, waited, no… said,

'Goes down easy.'

'Sneaks up on you, like the country itself. You wake in the morning, have a glass of water, you're pissed again.'

He moved to the bookshelf then carefully edged a volume out, looked at it with reverence, handed it to Porter, said,

'Get you started.'

It was one of the old Penguin editions, the green-and-white cover with:

Cop Hater

by

Ed McBain.

'Thanks, I'll take good care of it.'

Encouraged, Brant continued:

'Published in 1956, it's a winner. I've another fifty titles if you like that.'

Porter kept his appreciation low, the prospect of more was horrendous. He said,

'I'd better make a move. You still on for the wedding?'

'I'm on for anything.'

PART TWO

I feel like I'm fighting a battle
when I didn't start a war

Dolly Parton

RADNOR BOWEN WAS in the dumps after his meeting with Brant. He'd been so hopeful about his role as a snitch, believing it to be lucrative and reasonably safe. His knee still hurt from where Brant had manipulated him. The hope of decent payoff had been blown.

Radnor knew – all his instincts said so – that the cop killer was the case to break. There had to be serious money in it. He'd felt so down he almost didn't go to meet his contact: the guy from the gym he'd told Brant about, who knew a psycho who'd bragged about 'dealing with the police'. Radnor went because he had nothing else going and because he couldn't let go. There had to be an angle somewhere in this.

The guy, part-owner of the gym, was called Jimmy. He'd a bald patch, which he combed over, and a growing beer gut. Radnor thought he was a poor advertisement for his business. Not that he'd ever say so. Rule one of the 'Snitch's Handbook' was be ingratiating. Jimmy must have read his mind. He patted the stomach, said,

'Sign of prosperity, you know.'

Yeah, right.

They were in the Oval pub just after lunch, when trade hits a lull. So quiet that they could hear from the street:

'*Big Issue*, get yer *Big Issue*, help the homeless.'

Jimmy smiled, said,

'I'll have a pint of bitter and a ploughman's.'

Radnor got these, resenting the cost, cursing himself for this fool's errand. He had half a shandy, Jimmy dug into his food, said,

'So you want to know the head-case who near killed the gay guy?'

Radnor tried not to show too much interest lest money be mentioned. Jimmy was chewing with energy, said,

'I told all this to the copper who came by.'

Radnor knew who that was, nodded and Jimmy continued,

'A thick bastard, name of Brant. The fuck got a year's membership and wanted a free tracksuit as well.'

'What was the bloke's name who beat up the gay?'

'All in good time, Radnor. What's your hurry?'

He had to endure a further half hour listening to the difficulties of running a gym until, finally, Jimmy said:

'Barry Weiss. Here, I wrote down his address. I haven't seen him since. Not that I want to, he was definitely off the wall. Gave me the creeps, if you want to know the truth. Always smiling and if I know one thing, it's that nothing's that amusing. Our female members were always complaining about him.'

Radnor put the address in his pocket, acting as if it were of no consequence. Jimmy gave him an elbow in the ribs, said,

'So, you going to join the gym or what?'

❐

Having nothing better to do, Radnor had gone to the address and hung around. He was rewarded when Brant and Porter emerged, looking less than happy. A little later, a man came out; tall, with short blond hair, athletic build… and smiling. Radnor muttered,

'Hello, Mr Weiss.'

His heart rate had increased, the old surge of elation he'd had before he broke into a house. Radnor knew this guy was dirty. After thirty years in prison, he knew that facial expression, had seen it a hundred times in the yard – the smirk of someone who's put a shiv in a man from behind. What the smirk mostly said was 'I want you to know what I did and how much I enjoyed it.'

Grade-A psycho.

Radnor decided to follow him, carefully. Barry Weiss was taking no chances, changed direction a number of times as if he suspected a tail. Then hopped on a bus. Radnor barely made it. Each time they stopped, Radnor had to scan the path for Weiss, but he was getting a kick out of it. If the guy was going to this trouble, he was hiding something. Then the thought hit Radnor: Jesus, what if he's going to kill someone *now*?

Radnor had no illusions about heroics, no scenario of him tackling a well-built bloke like that. He'd have to make it up as he went along. Caught up in this, he nearly missed Barry getting off at Waterloo, had to scramble and as the bus moved off, the conductor shouted,

'No alighting when we're in motion.'

Radnor near twisted his ankle as he hopped from the bus. When he arrived at the station concourse, his heart sank. He'd lost him. Fuck, fuck, fuck. But then Radnor saw him, near the lockers. Radnor moved fast, ignoring the ache in his knee. Barry was opening a locker.

Radnor did a scan of the numbers: 68, okay. Now Barry was taking out a wallet, gazing at it, then putting it in his pocket, shutting the locker. Moving away.

Radnor passed by 68 and saw that the lock wasn't going to be a problem. He'd broken into houses with a hundred times that security. Saw Barry ordering coffee, chatting with the assistant, Radnor thought: Mr Affability.

Then he saw the assistant's face register horror and Barry took a seat, a satisfied smirk in place. Confirmed Radnor's impression of serious derangement. Ten minutes later, Barry was up and moving through the crowds, leaving the station. Radnor headed for the coffee shop, ordered an espresso. The girl still seemed shaken. Radnor, in his best non-threatening accent, asked,

'Are you all right, dear?'

She looked round, ensuring Barry was gone, said,

'A customer... showed me a photo of his family, three lovely children and his wife. When I admired them, he said they were all dead.'

'Oh, you poor girl, what an awful ordeal.'

Then she shook herself as if ridding herself physically of Barry's presence, said,

'This will sound terrible but I... I didn't believe him,

isn't that awful? I mean, I think he deliberately tried to scare me.'

Radnor wondered where they were on that espresso, the aroma from the beans had awoken a passion for a caffeine hit. He said,

'There are some weird people around, you have to be careful.'

'I will, you're very kind. What did you say you wanted, cappuccino?'

'No, double espresso, if you please.'

She glanced around again, said in a conspiratorial tone,

'I'll only charge you for a single, don't say anything.'

'My dear, I won't breathe a word.'

Sipping the coffee, he felt that the omens were good, improving by the minute. He thought: See, Brant. See what good manners and breeding achieve?

He felt as if he actually were from Hampstead.

Returning to Waterloo the next day, he gave the coffee shop a wide berth. He didn't want to adopt the damn girl. In his pocket, he had his 'Slim Jim': state-of-the-art tools that were light, flexible and invaluable. Though he had turned his back on his previous profession, he kept the implements of his trade. Some things were too valuable to relinquish. Approaching locker 68, he kept his face in neutral. CCTV cameras were everywhere and he didn't want to alert any watcher.

Taking the tools from his pocket, he used his right shoulder as a block to passers-by. After three minutes the door opened. A surge of pride in his abilities coursed through Radnor's body. He enjoyed the moment, then looked inside the locker. For a second, he didn't quite grasp what he saw, then exhaled a deep breath, said,

'Bingo.'

❐

The phone rang and Dunphy grabbed it. He hadn't heard from 'The Blitz' for a few days and hoped he hadn't retired, just when the story was reaching its zenith. He said,

'Yes?'

'Harold Dunphy?'

'Yes?'

'*The* Harold Dunphy? The crime reporter.'

Dunphy was well pleased. This was the type of recognition he'd been craving. Maybe he'd won an award, said,

'One and the same.'

Felt this was a good reply, confident and assertive, the answer of a guy who deserved prizes.

'Would you like to know who "The Blitz" is?'

Dunphy reached for his cigarettes, got one going, saw a tremor in his fingers, kept his voice low, said,

'That would be good.'

'Or, Mr Dunphy... how would you like to be the man who nails the fucker?'

Dunphy, inured to profanity, was taken aback. Until then the voice had been cultivated, modulated, Hampstead even, so the obscenity came as a shock. It confirmed Dunphy's instinct that it was genuine. When toffs cursed, it was for a good reason. He said,

'It would be an honour to bring him down.'

A pause and he wondered if he'd given the wrong answer, then:

'Well, Mr Dunphy, you have a think about how much of an honour it would be. In particular, how much you'd be willing to pay for such a privilege...'

'Oh.'

'Come, come, Mr Dunphy, did you think this was a citizen doing his bit?'

'I guess not.'

Click.

'That's sick,' said Barbara
'It's deranged.'
'It's psycho.'
'It's the... other sex.'
'Isn't it just the truth?' said Barbara.

Richard Rayner.
Los Angeles Without a Map

FALLS WORE A heavy black coat, buttoned to the chin. She pulled a white cap down over her hair. As she got into the car, Nelson gave her a quizzical look. She snapped,

'What?'

'Nothing, the coat… it's a good choice.'

'Like you'd know.'

As they pulled away, he asked,

'You want me to turn on the radio?'

'Take a wild guess.'

He left the radio off. The silence for the rest of the trip was lethal. Nelson ran through a number of topics he might broach but dismissed them all. Falls stared straight ahead, a red rose clutched in her fingers. All he hoped was she wouldn't want to cast it in the grave. The only concession she'd given was to forego the church ceremony and just meet the funeral party at the graveyard. Nelson parked at the gates, said,

'Maybe we should do the next bit on foot.'

For answer, she got out. They walked along a gravel path, their shoes crunching in the air. A large crowd was gathered, British National Party members in heavy attendance. A priest was intoning:

'Man has but a short time to live and is full of misery.'

171

Or words to that dire effect.

Nelson wanted to say,

'Cheerful bugger.'

But Falls' expression didn't encourage him.

They stood to the side of what appeared to be the principal mourners. A shabby couple, looking crushed, had to be the parents. Two BNP members helped the gravediggers lower the coffin. Then Falls stepped forward, laid the rose on top and moved quickly back. When the coffin was released, the priest said another few words and then the crowd began to disperse. Falls approached the parents, began,

'Your son was...'

The father put out his hand, to shield his wife from her, finished Falls' sentence with,

'No friend of the likes of you.'

And they turned, walked quickly away. Nelson grabbed Falls' arm, led her back to the car. He heard,

'Hey!'

And turned to see two skinheads approaching. He moved in front of Falls, braced himself. They had armbands with BNP on them. Falls noted with sadness how young and good-looking they were, though hate was already marring the freshness of their pallor. She could feel the hatred like a cold wave rolling towards her. They stopped a foot from Nelson, one of them put out his hand, threw the crumpled rose on the ground, said,

'We don't take shit from niggers.'

Nelson started to spring but she held him back.

The second one said,

'That black cunt got our comrade killed.'

And he spat, the spittle landing on the sleeve of her coat. Then they gave the Hitler salute and took off. Nelson let out his breath slowly, bent to retrieve the flower. She snapped,

'Leave it, it's contaminated.'

In the car, as they pulled away, she said,

'Stop at The Cricketers.'

'Okay.'

Took him a while to park and he could sense her impatience. As they got out of the cat, he said,

'You want to get some breakfast first?'

But she was already heading for the pub. Caught her up as she reached the counter. She ordered:

'Two large whiskies.'

Nelson looked at the guy then at Falls, said,

'I think I'll have coffee.'

'Then order it, these are for me.'

When the drinks came, she poured both into one glass, moved to a table. The barman, a sympathetic expression on his face, asked,

'A coffee?'

'Yeah.'

Nelson was tempted to simply turn on his heel and take off. Sighing, he headed for her table and she said,

'Don't sit.'

'What?'

'You've done your chaperone jaunt, now you can fuck off.'

'Falls, we need to talk.'

'Oh yeah, about what? Italian restaurants, or maybe how much of a man you are? How you treat a woman with respect and piss off the first night?'

He put the coffee down, said,

'If that's what you want. I'll call you, maybe?'

'I've been called enough for one day.'

As Nelson headed out, the barman raised his eyes to heaven.

❐

McDonald had to drag himself to work. He felt shattered. The hardboiled stance had deserted him as soon as the geek went out the window. How Brant maintained that role day in, day out, was a mystery. His own plan to track Brant, bring him down, was undergoing a re-appraisal. If Brant had done similar acts and was still a hard-ass, then he was a fucking ice man. McDonald shuddered when he thought of his pursuit of him. Jesus, what madness. Brant would have thrown him out the window and had takeaway chips after.

All night, McDonald had twisted in his bed. Each snatch of sleep brought the geek, covered in blood, his neck grotesquely altered. McDonald wondered if he'd ever sleep again. Plus, when the body was discovered, there'd be an investigation. Christ, what if he was caught? His fingerprints had to be all over the flat... and on the geek's glasses. He tried to shut down that line of speculation.

By the time he got to the station, he was worn out. The desk sergeant barked,

'What have you been at?'

Guilt danced all over him: did they know already? He stammered,

'W-h-h-hat?'

'Look at you, you have black circles under your eyes. What, were you clubbing?'

'No... I...'

'You'll need to get a grip, constable. Partying till the small hours is not a smart move if you've any ambition.'

'Yes, sarge.'

'You're for it this morning.'

'Oh?'

'Chief Inspector Roberts has been screaming for you. You're lucky to be with him, he's covered in glory these days.'

'Lucky? Yes, I'm lucky.'

'But not for much longer if you don't get your head out of your arse. Don't stand there like a prick, get going.'

He did.

Knocking on the door of Roberts office, he considered going,

'Argh...'

And hightailing it out of the station. Heard,

'Come in.'

Roberts was the picture of activity – fresh, crisp and energised. He asked,

'So, what happened?'

'Happened, sir?'

'At the bloody post office. You staked it out, didn't you?'

'Oh yes, sir, they were very helpful, provided a counter where I could observe without being seen.'

'And...?'

'And... ahm... nothing.'

Roberts shot to his feet.

'Nothing? Then how come another pensioner was attacked last night? And guess what, in a building that's not a bloody spit from the post office.'

*By the time you say you're his, shivering and
sighing
And he vows his passion is
Infinite, undying –
Lady, make a note of this
One of you is lying.*

Dorothy Parker

PORTER ALIGHTED FROM the cab outside Barkers deparment store. He had offered to pick up Brant who'd said,

'No, I'll be outside the church, having a smoke.'

He was.

But not alone. By his side was a woman. She was in her late thirties with straggly blonde hair, a very short mini and a face that had been walloped often. A black bomber jacket barely contained her huge breasts. Brant gave a wry smile. He was wearing a bespoke suit that said 'cash or blackmail', probably both. A white rose in his lapel gave a lopsided slant to the jacket. He said,

'This is Kim.'

She held out her hand, said,

'Charmed, I'm sure.'

Porter shook her hand, noting the rough feel. He said,

'We'd better go in.'

The ceremony was nearly over, the church crammed. Brant whispered,

'Jeez, they're in some kind of hurry, yeah?'

The groom was saying,

'Yes, I do.'

From Porter's position, the groom looked old, very old.

In contrast to the bride, dressed in white, who appeared scarcely out of her twenties. Brant leered at Porter, let his tongue loll from the side of his mouth. After the service, the newlyweds posed for photos outside the church. Later, they'd discover – to their horror – that Kim and Brant had crept into the pictures. Porter moved forward, congratulated his father then motioned to Brant and said,

'Dad, this is Sergeant Brant.'

Nash senior was staring at Kim and asked,

'Is this Mrs Brant?'

Brant, eying the bride, seemed not to have heard but then turned, said,

'No, she's a hooker.'

Nash swallowed, composed himself, said to Porter,

'I see, well, we must away. See you at the reception, with your... ahm... colleague.'

The Kensington Hotel was a short walk from the church. Kim moved to Porter's side with Brant walking point, she asked,

'The bloke who got married, is he really, like, your old man?'

'Yes, he is.'

He could smell her perfume and it was making him dizzy. Porter realised he couldn't think straight. For one awful moment, he felt she was going to link his arm. Now she asked,

'And your mum, doesn't she, like... mind?'

He laughed out loud, more from hysteria than humour. Brant said,

'See, Porter – you're having yourself a time.'
Porter glared, said,
'I'll talk to you later.'
Then back to Kim, answered,
'My mother is dead.'
'Oh, that's handy.'
Then she giggled, put her hand to her mouth, said,
'Oh my God, I didn't mean...'
'It's okay. How did you...' – he was going to say hook
up with – '...meet Sergeant Brant?'
More giggles, then:
'He found my name in a phone booth.'
Whatever else, Porter admired her total lack of shame.
They'd got to the hotel and she said,
'I'd love a Babycham, but not many places sell them
these days. Do you remember them?'
'Yes, I do.'
She settled for a vodka and white. Brant had moved
into the crowd and Porter wondered if he'd be stuck with
Kim for the day. She gave him an intense look, said,
'Don't worry, I won't be hanging out of you.'
'I didn't think...'
'Yes, you did. Men are so obvious. If they get crossed,
their faces get that tantrum expression.'
Her eyes scanned the crowd and she said,
'Believe me, I'm never alone long in a hotel.'

❐

The dinner was the usual rip-off: limp chicken and salad,

followed by dead dessert. No one was complaining, thanks mainly to the gallons of wine that were at hand. Then the speeches began, droning on for over an hour. Finally, Nash senior thanked his guests, near gushed about his beautiful bride and made no mention of his son. Porter checked his watch. Ten minutes tops, then he was leaving.

❏

Brant was chatting to the barman when Porter's father approached, said,

'Let me get you a drink, Sergeant.'

'Sure, a scotch will do it.'

They got that and Brant said,

'Chin chin, congratulations and all that.'

Nash was staring, said,

'You seem an unlikely person to be a friend of... my son?'

'How would you know?'

'Excuse me?'

'I could be wrong but I'd say you know fuck all about your son.'

Nash tensed, his body language moving into attack mode. Brant smiled and Nash willed himself to ease down, said,

'You surprise me, Sergeant, I wouldn't have taken you for a fag hag.'

Brant signalled to the barman for refills, asked,

'You'll be on that Viagra, yeah?'

Nash forced himself to smile though rage suffused him, said,

'That's a cheap shot, Sergeant.'

Brant waved a hand towards the crowd, said,

'Despite the flash hotel, you're a cheap kind of guy.'

Nash knew he should just walk away. He'd never be able to score points with this animal but a stubbornness kept him there and he tried another tack, said,

'I've been in business for a lot of years, I'm a pretty good judge of people. You ever get tired of being a flatfoot, you'd do well to consider the private sector.'

Brant finished his drink, took a step away from the bar, asked,

'Are you offering me a job?'

'A man like you, Sergeant, you'd do well.'

Brant seemed to be considering it and Nash decided to sweeten the pot, said,

'I'd help you find accommodation on this side of the river. You'd like it over here.'

'Tell you what, you ask anyone, they'll tell you. I'm an arsehole, but work for you? Even I'm not that big an asshole.'

'At my signal, unleash hell.'

Russell Crowe
Gladiator

RADNOR HAD ARRANGED to meet Dunphy at Waterloo, instructed,

'Wait in the station bar, have a copy of *The Tabloid* with you.'

'How do I know you'll show?'

'You bring the money, I'll show.'

Dunphy had discussed it with the editor who'd said,

'Do whatever it takes to clinch this, don't fuck it up.'

He was determined not to. The prospect of catching 'The Blitz' made his heart pound. If he played this right, he could be hearing from the quality papers, not to mention the perks. Sitting at the bar in Waterloo, he spread *The Tabloid* on the table, tapped the envelope in his pocket, a thick wad of notes there.

A man approached, wearing an old Crombie and a cravat. He was smiling, Dunphy asked,

'You're...?'

'The man you were expecting.'

He sat and Dunphy asked,

'What do I call you?'

'Your ticket to ride. Did you bring the money?'

Dunphy tapped his pocket, asked,

'What have you got for me?'

'Let's go, it's a visual.'

Radnor led the way to the lockers. Dunphy's excitement was building. Radnor glanced around, then opened number 68, said,

'Feast your eyes.'

Dunphy did. Then,

'Are these items what I think they are?'

'Trophies I believe is the term. Don't touch anything.'

Dunphy was already composing the headline:

Sick Killer's Souvenirs

He asked,

'And you know who this locker belongs to?'

'I sure do, saw him open it myself.'

Here was the tricky part. Dunphy tried to stay cool, asked,

'And when do I get the name?'

'Ah, some further negotiation is required.'

A hundred yards away, Barry Weiss watched them in horror, his mind racing:

What the fuck…? It's the reporter, the treacherous bastard, and the tall bloke, looking like some army fuck… Wait a minute, I know him… think, think, come on… yes, the Irish pub, talking to Brant. It was him; Jesus, he must have followed me.

He watched as the two men headed for the bar, to celebrate no doubt. At that moment he knew what he had to do. Kill them both. Negotiations were obviously going on, how much they'd buy and sell him for. A torrent of rage shook his body. If he'd had the Glock with him, he'd have walked right over there and settled their negotiations on the spot.

But which one to do first? Who posed the biggest threat? The snitch, yeah. He was the one with the information. Christ, it was going to be a busy day. As he watched, the snitch stood and walked to the toilet. Barry had a reckless idea and acted on it. Strode into the bar, passing right by the journalist, he could have reached out his hand, said,

'Guess who?'

Into the toilet, where the snitch was preening himself in the mirror. Barry hit him fast, hard enough to stun him, and dragged him into a stall. The snitch's eyes opened wide in recognition and he gasped,

'I haven't told him your name.'

'Why?'

'He hasn't paid for it yet.'

Barry could understand that, said,

'I'm not going to hurt you, I only do police, remember?'

A mad hope in Radnor's eyes and Barry asked,

'How'd you get on to me?'

The snitch seemed proud, said,

'I got your address from the gym in Streatham, where you'd hurt a guy. Then I just followed you.'

Barry nodded, said,

'Simple and smart.'

Then he grabbed Radnor's head, said,

'You're going to have to help me on this. It's a tight squeeze.'

Jammed his head into the bowl. It was a tight squeeze.

Barry thought: This is a hell of a way to do it.

Keeping Radnor's head under the water was a bitch and he bucked like a bronco. Barry, on his back, yelled,

'Ride 'em cowboy.'

Took a while. Eventually Radnor grew still and Barry hauled him out, propped him against the wall, said,

'You're full of shit.'

Went through his pockets, found the fat envelope, peeked, went,

'Oh yes.'

Then Radnor's wallet, containing his ID, Travelcard and a few quid. Barry straightened, looked at Radnor then walked out of the stall. The toilet was empty but he'd have to hustle. The journalist would be wondering at the delay. He came out of the toilet, he'd reached the door of the bar when the barman caught him, said,

'These toilets are reserved for our patrons.'

Barry kept his face averted, said,

'Well, they're a disgrace, all clogged up.'

He was moving, knowing he should have kept his mouth shut but the rush, *ah, the fucking jolt*. He went to the locker, aware of time being against him, cleaned it out, stuffing everything into a holdall. Then out to the back of the station, put the bag into a skip and managed to grab a bus to Kennington, using Radnor's Travelcard.

'I don't know about any theory,' he said, 'but not everyone would feel this way about someone who left them for dead.'
'You think it's odd?'
'Let's just say, it's unusual.'

John Smolens
Cold

THE BAR HAD been closed. Forensics were in the toilet and Radnor had been removed. Dunphy was sitting with his head in his hands, a large brandy on the table. Brant was standing and Porter was sitting, eying the journalist. He said,

'Tell me again what happened.'

'Jeez, how many times? Okay, he went to the toilet. When he hadn't returned after... I don't know, fifteen minutes, I got concerned, thought maybe he fell in.'

Brant said,

'He did.'

Dunphy, remembering his last encounter with Brant, automatically massaged his stomach. Porter asked,

'So then?'

'So then! So fucking then I went to see if he was all right, but he wasn't, someone had drowned him... killed the poor bastard in fucking Waterloo Station. How weird is that?'

Porter, making an intuitive leap, said,

'Ah, but Mr Dunphy, you didn't exactly come rushing out, did you?'

'What?'

'The barman says you were in there for at least five

minutes. In fact, he was wondering if you two didn't have a little something going on.'

Dunphy was outraged, glared at the barman who was polishing glasses, then:

'I... looked for the money.'

'Money?'

'Yes, the bloody paper's money. What we were paying this man for the exclusive.'

'And did you find it?'

Dunphy drained the brandy, signalled to the barman who said,

'No can do, mate. Can't you see we're closed?'

He turned back to Porter, his face red from the drink, said,

'The envelope was gone, I couldn't even find a wallet, Christ, I don't even know the poor bastard's name.'

Brant moved round to Dunphy's front, said,

'The poor bastard was Radnor Bowen.'

The brandy hit Dunphy's bloodstream, he peaked, suddenly remembered, went:

'The locker! Shit, go and check, you're not going to believe what's in there.'

Porter felt a wave of fatigue, said,

'How about you tell me?'

Dunphy recalled Radnor's face, the near joy in his eyes and repeated the snitch's words,

'It's a visual.'

'Not any more, it's empty.'

'What?'

Ken Bruen

'Yes, he topped Radnor, then casual as you like, cleaned out the locker, while you, Mr Dunphy, you were... what? Sitting here with your thumb up your arse.'

Dunphy was shaking his head, saying,

'Jeez, this guy is good. Talk about a set of *cojones*, like coconuts.'

Porter wanted to knock him off the seat, settled for:

'You might temper your admiration with the thought that he'll probably be coming for you next.'

Brant turned to the barman, said,

'You want to hit me with a double of some Irish.'

The barman continued to polish a glass, said,

'No can do, buddy. Like I told the dickhead, we're closed.'

Brant shot out his hand, catching the glass, leant half over the counter.

'Listen up, I'm only going to say this once: I am not your buddy and when I ask you for a drink, you go, "Ice with that, sir?" Now, let's begin again... a double Irish.'

'You want ice with that... *sir*?'

'Don't be ridiculous, who needs ice?'

The barman placed the drink carefully on the counter, said,

'That will be five quid, sir.'

Brant smiled

'Like you said, you're closed. Now, tell me again about the guy you had words with.'

'I was busy. Here it's always busy but I always spot the freeloaders – guys too cheap to pay for the toilet on the station, think they can sneak in, piss for free. I catch them every time.'

'You're a hero. Now, about this guy.'

'Clocked him going in and he was, like, ten minutes. That's how long the dopers take. You go in and they're already nodding. This guy comes out, big hurry but I caught him, gave him the speech.'

'Spare me the speech, what did he look like?'

'Big, like he worked out, set of shoulders on him.'

'And he was white?'

'Yeah, he was white.'

'Would you recognise him again?'

'No.'

'You're certain?'

Now the barman got to smile, moved out of Brant's reach, said,

'I saw what he did to the poor schmuck in the toilet. I definitely wouldn't recognise him again.'

When they eventually let Dunphy go, he asked,

'Will I be getting police protection?'

Brant said,

'We'll be all over you.'

Porter watched him go and Brant said,

'The wrong guy got drowned.'

They headed up to the Railtrack office, got hold of a guy named Hawkins who operated the CCTV. Porter said,

'We'll need the tapes for the past month.'

Hawkins' shoulders slumped, he said,

'I'd love to help but...'

Porter tried to stay calm, said,

'This is a murder inquiry, we...'

Hawkins hands were up, saying,

'There's no tapes.'

'What?'

'The cameras haven't been loaded for six weeks.'

'You're bloody joking! Why?'

'Cutbacks.'

'I don't believe it, jeez.'

Hawkins tried to smile, went:

'The public doesn't know. I mean, the cameras are still a deterrent, it's a psychological thing.'

Porter was close to boiling point:

'It's a bloody disgrace. A man was drowned in a toilet, the killer is swanning round the station, cameras everywhere and not one single picture. If that's deterrent, God forbid you ever decide to try encouragement.'

As they stormed out, Hawkins said,

'Don't blame me.'

Brant answered:

'But we do blame you and guess what? We'll remember you.'

'Ah, come on, you guys do the same thing.'

'What?'

'Con the public. They think the police are there, like the cameras, but it's bullshit.'

They hadn't an answer and kept going. TV crews were packed outside the bar. Dunphy, surrounded by reporters, was giving it large.

Brant said,

'He seems to be over his shock.'

'Yeah.'

'The barman said that the man leaving the toilet was big, athletic. Ring any bells?'

'Barry Weiss? It's a reach.'

'What else have we got?'

'Nothing.'

But Barry was gone, he'd moved without a forwarding address.

*Then her eyes dropped to the closely printed
page and she ran a long finger down the third
column until she reached the bottom. 'Hold on
to your Victorian values,' she cautioned,
'this is juicy stuff.'*

Loren D Estleman
Angel Eyes

WHEN BARRY OPENED the envelope he'd taken from Radnor, he said,

'Fuck me.'

Counted it twice to ensure it wasn't his imagination, then shouted,

'I'm out of here.'

He'd gone back to his flat at New Cross, packed a few items, looked round, roared,

'Bye, shit-hole.'

He caught a cab at the end of the road, said to the driver,

'Take me to Bayswater.'

The driver looked at him, said,

'Going to cost, pal.'

Barry leaned forward, asked,

'When I got in, did I go, "How much to Bayswater?"'

'No... but...'

'Or did I look like some limp dick who thinks Bayswater is down the road?'

'No, I just thought...'

'Yo' buddy, driving, that's what you do. If you could think, we wouldn't be having this conversation.'

That shut the guy up. Barry stretched back thinking:

Man, this is the life, I'm fucking master of anything I touch.

He felt like a god.

❏

He had the cab stop on Westbourne Grove, paid him, saying,

'I was going to tip you generously but I think you'll learn more from deprivation.'

The driver would normally have gotten out, whipped the guy's ass, but he'd seen the eyes and just wanted to get the hell away. Barry found a small hotel advertising long-term stays, just off the main road. He checked in and paid two weeks up front, said to the proprietor,

'I'm going to be happy here.'

When Bill Haley toured England and arrived by boat at Southampton docks, Tony Calder and his friends were waiting to greet him, dressed in their best teddy-boy gear:

'He came off the boat and the minute we saw him, someone shouted, "Fucking hell, he's old – he looks like my grandad." So we left and went home and we never played his records again, ever.

'ROCK AROUND THE Clock' was playing. Roberts looked at the pub owner, who said,

'It was on a batch of tapes I bought, I don't know what's on half of them. I think I heard The Shadows yesterday.'

Roberts brought the drinks over to the table. He'd asked Brant for a drink, catch up on stuff; Brant was listening to the track, said,

'Jeez, how old is that?'

'Not bad though.'

Then Roberts told him the story about Haley arriving in England and Brant said,

'The song is shite.'

The Tabloid was on the table, with the headline

Police Informant Murdered in Broad Daylight

Roberts nodded at it, said,

'Looks bad.'

Brant finished his drink, said,

'Bad! You should have seen Radnor, the poor fuck looked horrendous.'

'You're losing a lot of snitches.'

'They're getting greedy and that makes them careless. You know how it is, guv, get sloppy and you're history.'

Roberts thought about that. A new record was playing, sounded like 'Tie a Yellow Ribbon', he asked,

'What's the deal with you and Porter Nash?'

'Deal?'

'Yeah, I mean, you're not just working together, you're what's the term... tight?'

Brant's mouth turned down – a bad sign – and he said,

'I like the guy.'

'Hey, Sergeant, I'm not knocking it. Just it's so unlike you, especially with a gay. I thought you hated them?'

Brant grinned:

'I hate everybody.'

Roberts decided to let the subject drop, it wasn't going anywhere. Further probing and he'd sound like he was jealous or something. Instead, he asked,

'You have a suspect for the killings?'

'Yeah, a witness description matches a guy we'd already interviewed. We went round to his place but, hey, he's done a bunk.'

'Which would indicate guilt of something.'

'Yeah. If it's him – and it sure is looking good – he enjoys fucking with us. The locker at Waterloo was rented in the name of B Litz. "Blitz".'

'You have searches out for him?'

'Everywhere.'

'You want another drink?'

'Lots of them.'

❏

Barry had decided on a few drinks to celebrate his new location. Nothing major, just a few to chill out. But it got away from him and he lost count of how many he'd put away.

Leaving the pub, he couldn't believe it was dark. How'd that happened? Decided on a walk to clear his head. He was moving unsteadily by Hyde Park when the urge for a piss hit. Why the hell hadn't he gone in the pub? The park was closed so he did a quick look round then scaled the railings, near impaled himself. He'd got his zip down, was about to unleash when he heard,

'Hey, you.'

Turned to face a young policeman. He couldn't believe it, asked,

'What is it with you guys? Every time I take a piss, you appear. Don't you have any proper crimes to solve?'

Before the cop could reply, Barry's urge could wait no longer and the urine came flooding out, all over the cop's boots. Barry said,

'Oops.'

The cop looked at his shoes in disbelief, then:

'That's it, you're nicked.'

Barry moved back a step, said,

'Alas, you've caught me without my hammer.'

'What?'

'My signature, what I use to beat the fuck out of policemen.'

Realisation began to dawn on the young cop. He fumbled for the radio on his tunic and Barry lunged. When he'd the cop on the ground, his hands around the throat, he said,

'I'd hoped for a wee break but you lot keep coming.'

After, he tore the radio off – it was squawking like a parrot – and stomped it into the ground. Said,

'Shut up. How am I supposed to bloody think?'

As he came back over the railings, a group of tourists gawked at him and he shouted,

'I'm Jack The Ripper.'

They were still staring as he weaved his way towards Bayswater. He was beginning to wonder if this whole new start was all it was supposed to be.

❐

In the pub, Roberts had cut out early as a prospective buyer for his house had called. Brant had asked,

'You're moving?'

'Yeah.'

'Where to?'

'I have no idea.'

Brant, two pints to the good, phoned Porter, who arrived just after Roberts left. Brant said,

'Think I'll get rat-faced, want to join me?'

'I'll stay for one, but I have to get back. We're swamped in paper.'

Brant was getting into his stride, the pints going down easy. He asked,

'What if we find this guy and can't prove anything?'

'You mean Barry Weiss?'

'Yeah. Let's say we know it's him but can't touch him, what then?'

'Where are you going with this?'

Brant didn't answer for a time, then,

'You told me before about a paedophile you dealt with yourself, when he couldn't be got through the usual process.'

Porter hadn't touched his drink, seemed astonished, said,

'I thought you were asleep when I told you that.'

Brant smiled answered

'I was nearly asleep, does that count?'

'I'm not sure we should continue this line of talk, I don't like where it's going.'

Brant had finished his drink and reached over, took a belt of Porter's, said,

'The Clapham Rapist. He sort of fell on his knife, gutted like the pig he was. Falls... and others... suggested I helped him along. It's not something that I'd lose any sleep over.'

Porter stood up.

'I'm going to pretend we didn't have this conversation.'

Brant looking relaxed, almost happy, asked,

'You didn't answer my question. Would you let him continue slaughtering our guys?'

'You've been drinking, Brant. I'm going to clock it up to that, see you tomorrow.'

'You'll think about it, Porter, I know I will.'

Later, Brant switched to shorts and the tape had come

full circle, started up again. Brant concentrated with a drunk's ferocity and went,

'No, that song is still shite.'

The owner, who'd heard Bill Haley now at least thirty times thought: He's got a point.

The trouble with torture was people got carried away. You never knew when to stop. You completely forgot why you started destroying somebody with pain and you ended up putting paid totally to getting whatever it was you wanted out of them in the first place.

Peter Robe
Pig's Blood

McDONALD WAS IN the canteen – Gladys, the tea lady having a good look at him. He ordered poached egg on toast, she put the food before him, said,

'I've given you two eggs.'

'Thanks a lot.'

'You'd make a nice friend for that Porter Nash.'

McDonald stared at her, then:

'What the hell do you mean by that?'

'Nothing, just that you're both fine specimens of the male sex.'

He shoved the plate back at her.

'Keep the bloody eggs.'

He grabbed a tea and stomped to a table. Gladys watched him go, thought: They're so touchy, that lot.

McDonald was still fuming when Roberts came in and said,

'I need you.'

He was going to answer,

'Fuck off.'

But whined with,

'Can't I finish my tea?'

'Tea! You're stuck in here all day, aren't you sick of tea? Come on, we have a murder.'

When they got to the car pool, only a Volvo was available, so Roberts said,

'You still drive, I take it?'

As they pulled off, Roberts gave directions and McDonald felt a chill. Roberts shouted,

'For Christ's sake, watch the road.'

When they pulled up outside the flats, McDonald was sure his eyes would betray him. Roberts said,

'You'll know this place.'

'What?'

'From your stakeout. The post office is just down the road.'

'No.'

He wanted to say,

'I'll wait in the car.'

With a heavy heart, McDonald followed Roberts into the flats. They didn't go up the stairs but on through the hall, into the yard. Scene of Crime officers were finishing up and the pathologist was tearing off plastic gloves. McDonald was aware of a choking, rancid smell; he couldn't bring himself to look. The pathologist, Ryan, went way back with Roberts, asked,

'What's wrong with your constable? First time?'

Roberts turned to McDonald, said,

'Jeez, if you're going to be sick, don't do it here, you'll mess up the crime scene.'

McDonald rushed down the hall, got to the street and puked. A woman passing, said,

'Oh, for goodness' sake! Drunk this time of the

morning and you a policeman. I'm reporting you, what's your number?'

Sweat blinding his eyes, sick on his mouth, he went:

'Piss off.'

'Nice language for an officer of the law. I'm definitely reporting you.'

She had a pen and paper out, was jotting down the number. He was too weak to respond; all he could think of was poached eggs and felt fresh bile erupt. Roberts, behind him, said,

'Jeez, don't harass the neighbours.' Turning to the woman, he said, 'Don't worry, madam, I'll sort him out.'

When McDonald straightened up, Roberts asked,

'What's with you? You've seen bodies before.'

'It's... ahm... he seems so young.'

Roberts gave him a long look, then,

'I'm impressed. How could you tell that when the face's so wasted?'

McDonald in full panic mode, blurted,

'The clothes, what young people wear.'

Roberts was still staring, said,

'Unusual conclusion on such a short glimpse.'

'I'm trying to think like you, sir. You know, make intuitive leaps.'

'Some leap. Let's go take a longer look, see how much more you can leap.'

As they stood over the body, Roberts asked,

'What's your thinking?'

McDonald stared up at the window, said,

'I'd say he came out of that window, broke his neck in the fall.'

'Good deduction but did he jump or was he pushed? Come here, look at this.'

Roberts crouched and McDonald, fighting revulsion, followed: the face would fuel further nightmares. Roberts had a biro, using it as a pointer, said,

'The nose is broken, I'd say that was before the fall. We better go up, see what the score is.'

McDonald was relieved to be getting away from the body when Roberts added,

'Ryan said the fall didn't kill him instantly.'

'What?'

'The poor bastard was lying here, alive, for some time.'

McDonald wanted to grab him, fought for control, went,

'But... but you said he'd a broken neck.'

'Yeah, but it didn't kill him right away. He might even have pulled through if he'd been taken to a hospital.'

McDonald groaned and Roberts patted his shoulder.

'Don't take it so personally, you have to stay detached, hear me?'

'Detached? I'll try, sir.'

They reached the flat when Roberts said,

'One thing is sure, though.'

'Yes, sir?'

'It was one cold-blooded animal who let him die out there. This is one bastard we're going to nail, am I right?'

'Right, sir.'

Coke is a sexual, mental, physical blast-off.

Marc Bolan

FALLS WAS BACK on duty. As so many officers were tied up with the 'Blitz' business, she'd been assigned to Brixton. It had been a lot of years since she'd walked the beat there. For a time, 'High Visibility' – the policy of having the police seen on the streets – had been very effective. Then it was abandoned, due to lack of resources. The Super, incensed that she'd attended the funeral, said,

'She wants aggro? I'll give her bloody aggro, send her back to jungle-land.'

Most people in the area ignored her. If they wanted help, the police weren't the ones they turned to. A few had harassed her for being black, oppressing her own kind. The first few days, she'd been edgy, paranoid, angry. Dealt harshly with some illegal parking and traders, penny-ante stuff. Her second day, she busted a dope dealer. Caught him at the bottom end of the market. He'd turned out his pockets and, to her surprise, he'd been carrying coke – a lot of coke. She'd expected crack and maybe some weed. He'd said,

'You can't bust me, the shit's not mine.'

'You're carrying it.'

'This is high-grade charlie. I lose that, I'll get a cap in the head.'

Then he bolted.

She was too tired to pursue and chances were, she wouldn't catch him anyway. Intending to turn the stuff in later, she'd continued her beat. Late in the afternoon, a shoplifter had kicked her ankles and screamed abuse. Falls was trying hard not to think about Metal, how his face had looked in death. For a respite, she'd gone into a department store, used their bathroom. Locking herself in a cubicle, she'd let out a breath of bone-weariness. Felt the package in her pocket, took it out, unwrapped the paper. She knew the ritual: using the bowl as a support, she got out her nailfile, carved three lines, took a fiver, rolled it and snorted. Waited, then hit the next two.

Nirvana.

It hit her brain running, lit up the whole world, a rush of well-being enfolded her. She felt the cold drip down her throat and wanted to punch the door in delight. Bounced out of there with wings on her feet. A store detective asked,

'Is everything okay, officer?'

She gave him a brilliant smile, said,

'Everything is beautiful.'

The man, in all his years on the job, had rarely seen a cop smile and he'd never seen one smile in Brixton. He wondered what she was on.

Coke users say that no subsequent hit ever equals the first. Ever after, it's always the pursuit of that first, unequalled high. Falls could vouch for that. The rest of the week, she snorted at regular intervals and though it was a rush, it was never *that* rush. She told herself,

'Soon as I finish this batch, that's it, put it down to experience and move on.'

She couldn't.

Busted a drug dealer's pad in Coldharbour Lane and as she confiscated the dope, said,

'I'm going to let you off with a caution.'

The dealer, who knew his market, stared at her inflamed nostrils and jerky movements, said,

'Getting yourself a little habit, officer?'

She clipped him on the side of the head. Later, she was horrified.

'I hit him! What is happening here?'

She upped her intake.

❒

There's an after-hours club near the Railton Road called 'The Riff'. They don't advertise, as there's no need. Frequented by both sides of the law, it's a neutral zone where the usual business is on hold. Cops liked it because they could drink till dawn and it was cheap. The villains liked it for much the same reasons, plus that they got to gauge the cops. There was rum or rum and coke to drink. Nobody seemed to mind. Round three in the morning, a little weed appeared and kept the proceedings mellow. Nelson had been going there recently. Since the disaster with Falls, he was consumed with her. So, instead of heading home, he went to the club. The war stories distracted him. He found he was developing a taste for rum.

A Rasta called Mungo sometimes sat with him, talked

about football. Once he'd offered Nelson a spliff, saying,

'Chills you way down, man.'

'I'm chilled enough.'

Friends would be stretching the terms of their contact but they were easy in their banter. This evening, Mungo seemed agitated. Nelson said,

'Maybe you should do one of your funny cigarettes.'

'I got me a problem, man.'

'You want to tell it?'

Mungo grew more nervous, glanced round, said,

'This club we got here, it works right?'

'Seems to.'

'Yeah, like we got's both side of the street, man. Nobody too uptight about their calling, like we got ourselves a demilitarised zone.'

Nelson smiled – the description fit – thought at least fifty per cent of the patrons were heeled. Carrying everything from knives through bats to shooters. He had a blackjack in his inside pocket. You drink late in Brixton, you need more than an attitude. Mungo misunderstood the smile, protested,

'This is a good vibe, man; no strutting your stuff in here, no posing.'

'You want to cut to the chase?'

'Like, I'm getting there bro', just so's you know I'm not, like, infringing on borders, you know what I'm saying?'

Nelson had no idea where this was going. Truth was, he had a buzz on – the rum, especially with coke, went down smoothly. You're sitting there, sipping and next thing, you're getting shit-faced. It crept up on a person, in a pleasant fashion. He wasn't sure he wanted Mungo to lay a downer on him, said,

'Hey, let's forget it. What about another drink?'

'Man, I don't want to bum you out but there is serious shit happening.'

Nelson rubbed his eyes, went,

'I'm listening.'

'A cop is taking down dealers.'

'What?'

'Yeah, ripping off the product, man. People is getting concerned. Some of these dealers, they're, like, serious folk. You fuck with them, they get biblical, even with a cop – especially a wo-man.'

'Whoa, back up, let me see if I'm getting this? A female police officer is taking down dealers?'

'That's it bro', and she a sister too.'

Took Nelson a moment to join it up, alarm bells ringing in his head, he asked,

'You got a name?'

'Falls.'

I felt like the top of my head was going right round. Terrifying, and ten minutes later, I'd put coke up my nose. That's how bad it was... You get up in the morning and the mirrors covered in smears of cocaine and the first thing you do is lick the mirror.

Elton John

BRANT AND PORTER WENT through Barry's flat like a tornado. Porter said,

'This guy is smart, nothing incriminating.'

Brant held up a series of photos, said,

'Likes himself, though. Half a dozen snaps here.'

'Take them.'

When they got back to the station, the news had broken about the young policeman in Hyde Park. Brant said,

'Let's go public with Barry.'

'You think?'

'Least we'll find the fuck.'

The *Six O'Clock News* carried the photo, asking Barry Weiss to urgently contact the police. Barry, in a drunken stupor, missed the broadcast. The cab driver, sitting in a pub, went,

'I know him.'

Called it in. By nine, an army of police were combing the hotels of Bayswater and Paddington and, by 10.30, had a hit. Porter got a call, inviting him along for the bust. When he and Brant arrived, the street had been cordoned off. Armed police were in the hotel lobby, led by an officer named Thomas. He knew Porter from their Kensington days, asked,

'How are they treating you in the sticks?'

'Like visiting royalty.'

Thomas gave Brant the once-over, said,

'Yeah, I bet. Your boy is in room 28. The manager says he hasn't moved since returning late this afternoon, apparently the worse for wear, drink-wise. We have a passkey and are ready to go.'

He handed the key to Porter, who turned and walked towards 28. Brant, on his right, suggested,

'Take him down fast, make sure he stays there.'

Porter nodded, listened at the door, inserted the key, turned it, opened the door slowly. Darkness. Moved a step into the room, found the light switch, flicked it on and moved aside as the stampeding troops rushed in. Barry, unconscious amid tangled sheets, was pounced on by a half-dozen men, handcuffed and thrown to the ground, Brant looked in the bathroom, shook his head. Barry opened his eyes, went,

'What the fuck?'

And got a slap in the mouth, a wallop to the balls. Porter said,

'Get him out of here, tear the room apart.'

Barry managed to croak,

'Some fucking clothes guys, please?'

He was wrapped in a blanket, bundled out fast. Porter let his shoulders sag as Brant surveyed a mound of cash on the bureau, he said,

'If we can link this to Dunphy's payment, we're on our way.'

Thomas moved out of the room and Porter followed, saying,

'Thanks.'

'You think he's the guy?'

'I don't know. Jeez, I hope so.'

'We'll take him to Kensington, you can have first crack at him.'

On the street, a crowd had gathered and they alternately jeered and applauded. Brant said,

'I love showbiz.'

❒

Falls was in her bathroom, afraid to look in the mirror. She couldn't believe how fast she'd come to total reliance on the drug. So, okay, she'd been hurting: the loss of Rosie, Nelson's rejection, then the murder of Metal – who'd be able to walk unhurt from that? The coke had been just a pick-me-up, get those first Brixton days done. She'd begun to anticipate the new day, getting out there, getting high.

A shudder ran along her spine. All she thought about was the white powder and the dread of running out. Sure, she'd cut a few corners to get hold of it but let's not dwell there.

A pounding at the door. She ignored it, hoped they'd go away. Got louder and sounded like the door would come in. Dragged herself to open it. Nelson, looking like he was about to have a seizure. She said,

'Go away.'

And tried to close the door. He shoved and she fell backwards as he came marching in. Getting shakily to her feet, she said,

'What the hell are you doing?'

Before he could answer, a voice came from the bedroom:

'What's all the noise?'

They both turned to see a skinny white guy, in his twenties, dressed in loose grey Y-fronts. He looked like a roadie after a rough gig. Nelson moved, pushed past him and gathered up clothes from the bedroom floor, the guy going,

'I'm getting some negative vibes.'

And was grabbed by Nelson, hustled to the door, flung into the street, his clothes sailing behind. He yelped,

'I need a caffeine fix, man.'

The door was slammed. Nelson turned to face Falls, said,

'The state of you, like some crack junkie and with that…'

He pointed to the street, adding,

'Trailer trash. What the hell do you think you're playing at?'

She had to get something, said,

'I need the bathroom.'

Got in there and tried to get a grip, thinking: Okay, take it slow, do two lines then get out there, deal with that bully, yeah, that's the best thing.

Had the lines laid on the cistern, was about to snort when the door came crashing in, Nelson towering above her, saying,

'Aw Jesus, on your knees, scrambling to get that shit.'

He moved, swiped the powder away, grabbed her arm and hauled her back to the living room, threw her into an armchair. She tried,

'You can't do this, who do you think you are?'

He moved right in her face, she could smell toothpaste and the remnants of... rum? He spoke through clenched teeth:

'Who am I? I'm the cop who can bust your ass for possession, for intent to distribute, for extortion... you want me to continue? We're talking eight years jail time, and that's minimum. Now do you know who I am?'

She tried to gather her thoughts. How did he know all this? Couldn't meet his eyes. Nelson backed off, sank into the chair opposite. She searched his face for some softening but he looked like he hated her. She asked,

'What had you in mind?'

'You have a choice. You can go to jail or rehab.'

'Rehab?'

'Yes, right now, they're expecting you.'

He looked at his watch, continued,

'In fact, you're already late and they get very stroppy about that so you're off to a bad start. I hadn't expected you to be entertaining guests.'

She'd have killed for a line, her body was starting to tremble. She asked,

'This rehab, how long would I be there?'

'As long as it takes.'

'I can't, Nelson. I'm the type they'd mangle, I'm not cut out for that.'

'Fine.'

He stood up, headed for the door. She called:

'Wait, where are you going?'

'To shop you. The warrant will probably be handed down quickly, you being a cop and all. Let me guess — they'll come for you this evening, so you have... ten hours to coke out or... you could run.'

Tears formed but she steeled herself, said,

'I'll go.'

'Hey, you're not doing me any favours, I don't give a toss what you decide. You're a rogue cop, that's the bottom of the fucking barrel.'

'What do you want, blood? I'll go.'

'It's now, Falls. You pack some things, we're moving in five minutes.'

They were. He'd stood over her as she got a bag, no hope of a line. In the car, she asked,

'Where is it?'

'Croydon, a place called Fern House. I'm not going to lie to you, it's a tough project, you'll be put through your paces.'

'And you know the place... how?'

'The woman who runs it, I did her a favour once.'

Nelson was making good time, cutting through traffic, hitting all the green lights, gliding smoothly. Falls had hoped for a long, slow journey, finally pleaded:

'Couldn't we stop for a drink? I'm coming apart here.'

He took a quick look, said,

'No.'

Ten minutes later, they pulled into a quiet street, in front of a large imposing house. Falls stared then asked,

'That's it?'

'Yeah.'

He was about to get out when she touched his arm, said,

'I need a promise.'

'Depends.'

'Promise me you won't ever tell me why they call it Fucking Fern.'

A
dead
ringer
for love

PORTER, BRANT, ROBERTS and the Super were sitting round a conference table. Porter said,

'We've got him in the interview room.'

And he nodded at Brant, who said,

'I got hold of the *Big Issue* guy who said he saw the WPC being capped at the Oval. His identification would have given us all we needed but he says he can't remember: no way could he make a positive ID. We can't prove that the money from Dunphy is what we found in Weiss's hotel room. In conjunction with harder proof, we might have been able to make it look bad but not on its own.'

The Super was looking frustrated, said,

'What else do we have?'

Porter shifted through his files, said,

'A sharp medical examiner noticed the bullets that killed the WPC were similar to those he took from a traffic warden a few weeks earlier.'

The Super was lost, went,

'A bloody traffic warden, what the hell does that mean?'

Porter paused, then,

'It means he was practising.'

'What?'

'Working his way up to a policeman... or woman.'

The Super felt it was time to establish his leadership, show them how real results were achieved, said,

'We're going to pull the old con on Mr Weiss.'

Porter didn't like the sound of this. The Super was animated:

'The old tricks are the best ones. None of your fancy west London stuff needed here; we put a ringer in the cell with Weiss.'

Porter's heart sank.

'A ringer?'

'A policeman. Weiss will spill his guts.'

Before Porter could protest, Brant said,

'And you've someone in mind, sir, to play... the ringer.'

The Super, feeling his leadership was intact, said,

'PC McDonald, an up-and-coming officer, the new face of policing. Plus, he's street-smart.'

Porter looked to Brant for help but he remained expressionless. The Super continued:

'Right then, Porter, you can begin interrogation of the suspect and I'll arrange for McDonald to be nicked.'

He seemed amazed his joke fell flat.

❐

Barry Weiss was sitting in the interview room. Despite the hangover, he was making plans, told himself,

'Admit to nothing and they can prove nothing.'

The door opened and Porter came in with Brant. They sat down and Porter said,

'We're going to tape this, OK?'

Barry seemed to consider, then,

'I'll need to know who wins *Big Brother*.'

The first session lasted two hours and they got nothing. Barry asked for a lawyer and a Diet Coke, saying,

'I've got to count those calories.'

During the second session, Barry had tea and sandwiches, said,

'The bread's stale.'

A lawyer came and instructed Barry to say nothing. Barry stared at him, asked,

'How bright are you?'

They could hold him for 48 hours, then they'd have to charge him or release him. When Porter finally said,

'Take him to a cell.'

Barry said,

'Is that your final answer?'

He was surprised to find the cell occupied, asked,

'Don't I get one on my own?'

And got shoved inside.

The Super had briefed McDonald:

'This is your big break, laddie. All eyes are on you. I don't have to emphasise the magnitude of this case. Crack this and you're made.'

'Yes, sir.'

McDonald had been relieved to get away from Roberts. The strain of pursuing the geek murder had been enormous. If he did well now, he might never have to work with Roberts again. The Super was saying,

'You want him to confess. Don't be pushy or he'll smell a rat. Let him come to you. Admit to various crimes slowly. You have to appear almost disinterested so he'll try to impress you. He's a psycho, he'll want to boast, let you know how superior he is. Any questions?'

'I have the gist, sir.'

The Super appeared loath to stop, then,

'They didn't want you.'

'Sir?'

'Porter Nash, Brant, Roberts, they said you were the wrong man for the job. Are you, McDonald, are you the wrong choice? Have I made a grave mistake in entrusting this to you?'

McDonald felt like he was being briefed for *Mission: Impossible*, kept his face solemn, answered,

'I won't let you down, sir.'

'See you don't.'

He was wearing old jeans, a torn sweatshirt and scuffed trainers. There were two bunks in the cell and he settled in one, made as if he was sleeping. By the by, he heard commotion. They were bringing Barry down, heard him bitching about sharing a cell, then they pushed him in. The door clanged shut and it was quiet, save for Barry's breathing, heard:

'Hey, you.'

And his bunk was kicked. He took his time, turned, came awake, rubbed his eyes, asked,

'The fuck you want?'

Barry was gauging him, assessing his build, said,

'Let me introduce myself.'
McDonald stared and Barry went,
'Don't you get it? Intro to "Sympathy for the Devil"?'
'You woke me up.'
'Sorry about that, I've had a rough day.'
McDonald nodded, said,
'I'm Pete.'
'Well hello, Pete. What you in for?'
'A bit of GBH.'
Barry's eyes lit up; he asked,
'Yeah, who'd you batter?'
'Some tosser in a pub.'
'That's it?'
McDonald allowed himself a small smile, said,
'Perhaps one or two other items.'
'Like what?'
'Oh, a robbery they're hot on.'
Barry was having fun. His crime books had mentioned this type of scenario. They plant a cop and get you to fess up. This guy was so bad at it, Barry wanted to laugh out loud. Climbed on his bunk, said,
'Night, night.'
McDonald felt a panic build, asked,
'And... what about you?'
'Moi?'
'Yeah, what are they trying to stick you with?'
'Nothing much.'
'Must be something.'
A pause, then:

'Oh, yeah, I forgot to pay my TV licence but I'm going to front it out, know what I mean?

McDonald was nearly asleep when he heard,

'Pete?'

Disorientated, he didn't answer, heard,

'Pete, you awake, buddy?'

Realised he was 'Pete', went,

'Yeah, I'm awake.'

'Here's a question, you listening?'

'I'm listening.'

'It's more a supposition, you with me? Okay, here it is: a stone psycho, a cop killer is celling with a... cop. His speciality if you will, cops being who he kills. My question is, how good is this cop going to sleep?'

McDonald tried to keep his interest low, sound almost bored, asked,

'You want to tell me something, Barry?'

'You're asking the wrong question.'

'I am?'

'Sure, the question should be, did they set me up?'

'What?'

'The brass – they need a result, so you put a disposable cop in with the killer. They figure the guy has no control. You leave a policeman overnight with him, hey, he'll off the fuck. I mean, come on, it's what he does, he can't help it. The crime books call it the "Irresistible Impulse". They need a result and badly, the Press are on their backs, here's a guaranteed winner.'

McDonald couldn't see clearly: was Barry lying

down... or crouched on the bunk, what? He fought the screaming in his head, the desire to peep out of bed, see where the hell Barry was. He asked,

'You think I'm a policeman?'

No answer. Then a little later, he heard low laughter, a suppressed set of... giggles? Any chance of sleep was shot to hell. Sure, the guy was doing a number, fucking with his head, but he'd killed, what... six people, how conducive to sleep was that?

Bitter experience showed that in their sad country, whistleblowers rarely achieved anything more than their own destruction.

Marshall Browne
The Wooden Leg of Inspector Anders

BRANT AND PORTER were debriefing McDonald. Brant went:

'Christ, you look a mess. What is that, method acting?'

McDonald glared at him and Porter asked,

'Did you get a result?'

'He's the one, he did the murders, it's definitely him.'

'He confessed?'

McDonald shifted nervously, said,

'No, but it's him, he let me know that.'

Brant moved close, right in McDonald's face, said,

'He sussed you, didn't he? What did you do, show him your warrant card?'

McDonald looked away, then,

'Yeah, he sussed me.'

Porter slammed the table.

'Aw, for heaven's sake.'

McDonald wanted to explain – the fear he'd felt, what it was like to be locked up in close proximity to that animal – but these weren't the people to whinge to, so he just lowered his head.

Porter said,

'We're going to have to release him.'

McDonald near shouted:

'You can't, the guy is a total psycho, he enjoys the whole deal.'

Brant had a cold expression, said,

'Your boss is waiting for you.'

'The Super?'

Now Brant was smiling.

'I don't think he's going to be pleased, you being his golden boy.'

McDonald didn't want to let it go, tried,

'But you must do something, you can't just let him walk.'

Porter waved his hand in dismissal. After McDonald had left, Brant said,

'How much longer have we got?'

Porter looked at his watch, said,

'Nine hours. His lawyer's on the countdown already. What do you say we interrogate him some more?'

'Yeah, what else is there?'

❒

As McDonald approached the Super, he saw the hope in the man's face. Without thinking, he began to shake his head, the Super going,

'What's that mean? Shaking your head, that better not be what I think it is; you'd better have very good news.'

'I'm sorry, sir.'

'Sorry! What the hell is sorry? How could you screw it up? You had a golden chance and you blew it. Plus, I've had a complaint against you.'

'A complaint, sir?'

'From a member of the public. She says you were not only drunk while in uniform but you used offensive language. I'd have let it slide, covered for you, it's what I do, take care of my people, but you… You've made me look bad. You're suspended pending an investigation, without pay. You'll be lucky to hold on to your job.'

'But, sir…'

'Get out of my sight.'

Minutes later, McDonald was outside the station, bone-weary, not sure what to do. Porter spotted him and took a moment, said,

'Don't take it too hard.'

McDonald had a glazed look, said,

'Someone should off him.'

'The Super?'

'That animal in the cells, Barry Weiss. If he walks, someone should do him.'

Porter looked around, moved closer, said,

'Whoa, take it easy. You don't want to let people hear that kind of talk.'

McDonald let out a high-pitched laugh, asked,

'What'll they do, suspend me?'

He headed home, to his bedsit in Lewisham. He'd thought it was functional, efficient and merely a step on the ladder. Now he viewed it as a step on the way down. He tore off his clothes, emitting obscenities as the recent events replayed in his mind, asked himself,

'When did I last eat, am I hungry? Am I fuck.'

And climbed into bed.

'Suspended without pay'; the unfairness caused him to toss and turn till he fell into a fitful sleep, dreaming of Barry Weiss, with the Super's voice and the geek's clothes. The phone dragged him awake. He was covered in sweat, said,

'What...?'

The phone had that insistent shrill that warns:

'Don't answer, you'll be sorry if you do.'

He answered, heard,

'McDonald!'

'Yes.'

'This is Roberts, where the hell are you?'

Without thinking, he told the truth; always a bad idea, especially for a policeman, went,

'I'm in bed.'

'Jeez, get the hell up, I've good news.'

'Yeah, sir?'

'I know who killed our student.'

McDonald felt a shudder, said,

'I'm suspended, sir, without pay. The Super...'

'Bollocks. I'll sort it out, get down here.'

Click.

In Morita Therapy, the principle is: be scared to death – and do what you have to do.

FALLS WAS SCARED. The first few days were detox. Those days were a blur: she was crying out for a line or medication, anything to numb the pain. The doctor said,

'If it's not absolutely necessary, we don't use medication. You are addicted emotionally, your body isn't yet physically dependent. We caught it in time. Another week, who knows? Despite what you might think, it's better in the long haul that you don't have tranquillisers.'

Falls glared at him, said,

'Easy for you to say. I'd risk medication if it's no skin off your nose.'

He gave a tolerant smile – part contempt, part pity – said,

'The best thing is lots of water, food and vitamins.'

He was holding her chart, asked,

'You're a policewoman?'

'Yeah.'

'Mmmmm.'

Roughly translated, that means 'You sad bitch'. She said,

'What?'

'Well, I was wondering, isn't it a tad awkward, in your line of work, being an addict?'

She was beginning to think: How bad could prison be?

And answered,

'A tad awkward, yes, that describes it.'

On the fourth day, Mrs Fox, the one who called the shots, said,

'Elizabeth, you're going into population today.'

Falls couldn't remember telling her her first name, asked,

'Population?'

'Yes, you'll be sharing a room with Emily, taking your place in the house.'

'Lucky me.'

Mrs Fox had the benign face they construct in therapy school. It said:

'I've heard everything and nothing shocks me. More than anything else, I love you, you worthless piece of shit.'

And she had the voice to accessorise it. A quiet monotone that suggests depth, compassion and spirituality Mostly it bugs the bejaysus out of you. Now though, there was a slight chill as she chided,

'No one likes sarcasm Elizabeth. It won't facilitate your passage.'

'Yeah, right.'

Falls was shown a bright room with two beds. Mrs Fox said,

'Emily is at group. For the next four days, you are on probation.'

'And that means what exactly?'

'You don't watch television, read newspapers, make or receive telephone calls.'

Falls sat on the bed, said,

'You really get off on this, don't you?'

The benevolent smile deepened.

'It's usual to be resentful at this stage, Elizabeth.'

'Stop calling me that.'

The expression flickered then clicked back into place and she continued:

'To qualify for privileges, you have to earn them.'

Falls decided to try a smile of her own, asked,

'And whose ass do I kiss to earn them, apart from yours, of course?'

'Cooperation and honesty, that's all we ask, plus a complete willingness to join in the spirit of the house.'

'To be part of the team?'

'In a manner of speaking, yes.

As Falls didn't ask any more questions, Mrs Fox turned to go, then:

'We have made one exception in your case.'

'I can't wait to hear it.'

'Detective Inspector Nelson, a special friend of our community has asked to visit you this evening. On this occasion, we've bent the rules and he'll be here at seven.'

After she'd gone, Falls was surprised to feel she was looking forward to the visit. But then, what else had she going? Nothing.

The door opened and a woman entered. She was skinny, in her early twenties, with very thin, red hair and a pasty complexion. Put her hand out, said,

'I'm Emily.'

Falls took her hand, which was clammy, no strength in it. If she'd squeezed, she'd have crushed the bones, said,

'Hi, Emily.'

The woman closed the door, said,

'Sh... sh...sh.'

'Okay.'

Then went to the window, looked out, came back to Falls, whispered:

'I've got us a surprise.'

'You do?'

Produced a bar of chocolate, said,

'I'm going to split it with you.'

'Thank you.'

With concentrated precision, she broke the bar evenly, handed over a wedge, said,

'This is as good as an orgasm.'

Falls didn't have a reply to this, who did? Emily was examining her, said,

'I don't know any black people.'

Falls considered a variety of hard-ass replies – but hey, the girl was sharing – so,

'Well, us black folk, we sure do like our chocolate, so you've learnt one thing.'

Emily smiled, her teeth awash in chocolate, said,

'You'll be the only coloured person. We had an Asian guy but I don't think that's the same. What are you here for?'

'Dope.'

'Me too, and shoplifting, that's my favourite thing.'

Falls debated mentioning her profession, decided to wait, asked,

'How does it work here?'

Emily rolled her eyes, then:

'They like to break you down, get you to admit being worthless, then they rebuild you with all sorts of positive shit. The guy to watch out for is Alan: he specialises in confrontation, getting you broken, weeping and purging. I hate him, he's about five-foot nothing and looks like he never saw the sun in his life.'

Falls had finished the chocolate, felt the tiny hit from the sugar rush, went,

'Wait a sec, you're telling me some white midget is going to bust my balls?'

Emily was delighted, clapped her hands, asked,

'You ever do "vike"?'

'Vike?'

'Vicodin, a massive painkiller, it covers you in a cloud of bliss. Oh, it's like you'll never hurt again.'

Falls felt a wave of affection for this awkward, pasty-faced white girl, asked,

'That's your gig, getting away from hurt?'

Emily's eyes widened, she answered,

'Isn't everybody?'

'Not with Vicodin and most of them out there, they like to cause the pain.'

Emily was nodding as if she'd never heard of such a notion, said,

'You're smart, aren't you?'

'If I'm so smart, how come I'm in here, faking an orgasm on chocolate?'

She said, 'Did he suffer?'
I thought for a minute. 'He experienced terror.'
'No, I mean, did it hurt him?'
'I don't think so.'
'Too bad.'

Mary-Ann Tirone Smith
An American Killing

AS BARRY WEISS was being released, an air of doom pervaded the station. The cops had lined up, in silent rows, to watch him leave. Barry's lawyer glanced at them nervously, said,

'The sooner we get you out of here, the better.'

Barry, completely relaxed, asked,

'Are the Press waiting?'

'Reams of them. You want to cut out the back?'

Barry looked at him in astonishment.

'Are you nuts?'

He smiled at the officer who handed over his possessions, including the money, said,

'Hope it's all there.'

He didn't get an answer so Barry said to the lawyer,

'Count it.'

'What?'

'You heard me.'

'Christ, can't it wait?'

'Count it.'

He did and, nervous, missed the tally, had to restart. Barry said,

'You're too tense, need to lighten up.'

Finally it was done and the lawyer said,

'Let's get the hell out of here.'

'Not yet.'

'Not yet?'

'I've a few words for the troops.'

'Jesus, you want to be lynched? Let's go.'

Barry turned to the line of cops, said,

'I'm going to miss you guys. Despite the circumstances surrounding my stay – and I do appreciate it was difficult for you lot – I want to say there are no hard feelings. I'm not the type to harbour a grudge...' – here, he allowed himself a small chuckle and the line of cops stirred – 'So, when I sue your collective asses, I want you to remember, it's nothing personal. I'm not one of those—'

The lawyer grabbed his arm and pulled hard. Barry said,

'Hey, I'm not finished.'

'Yes, you are.'

And hustled him to the door. The front was reinforced plate glass and they could see the crowd of reporters.

Brant and Porter were standing at the threshold. Barry said,

'See you, dudes.'

Brant looked at him, smiled. Barry said,

'What are you smiling at, cocksucker? You screwed up.'

Brant winked and the lawyer manoeuvred Barry outside. The pack moved forward, microphones and questions storming in their faces. A man brushed his way to the front, said,

'Barry, I'm Harold Dunphy from *The Tabloid*. We'll

give you an exclusive deal, put you up in a hotel, reward you handsomely.'

Barry smiled, looked to his lawyer who shrugged. Dunphy, seizing the moment went on:

'We have a car waiting. Why give it away for free to… these…?'

Barry was tripping, said,

'You've got a deal.'

Dunphy gave a signal and two burly minders appeared, carved a way through the crowd towards a car. The Press were frustrated, cries of:

'Give us a quote, Barry.'

'Did you kill those policemen?'

Barry paused at the door of the car, turned to face them, grinned, said,

'No comment.'

FALLS WAS READYING herself for the therapy session. Emily, agitated, said,

'Alan will be gunning for you.'

'Thanks for warning me.'

'He'll do it in this session, when it's your first group. He likes to let you know from the off, take you down straight away. He makes people cry, degrades them in any way he can. He calls it levelling, to get you focused.'

'Don't worry, Emily, it'll be okay.'

The woman seemed unconvinced, almost close to tears, said,

'I'd hate to see him belittle you and I just know it's going to be bad.'

'Bad?'

''Cos you're pretty. I hope you don't mind me saying so, but it's true. And he gets rabid when the women have looks, as if he's punishing them. My first time, he didn't bother too much, just did the basic humiliation. That's 'cos I'm plain... No, don't say anything, I don't mind.'

Falls put her hand out, said,

'You've nice eyes.'

And laughing, they headed for therapy.

The group were already gathered, armchairs in a circle.

Two were vacant. Emily moved to one, Falls stood as the group assessed her. She clocked Alan immediately, his chair a little back from the others. The chair beside him was vacant, he was glancing through a file, didn't look up, said,

'Sit down.'

The tone was brisk, it conveyed 'don't fuck with me'.

She took the chair and was assailed by his aftershave. A thick, cloying scent, it made her want to gag.

He still hadn't looked at her. He was wearing combat pants, sweatshirt and trainers. The uniform of the relaxed therapist, a small stud earring in his left ear. There wasn't a sound in the room. The group was evenly divided between the sexes, ages ranging from late teens to over-sixties. What they shared was a cowed look. Alan cleared his throat, said,

'All right, people?'

The group responded:

'All right, Alan.'

The unity of the response startled Falls. Alan waited, then:

'Any infringements?'

A hand went up and he nodded; a middle-aged man said,

'I'm Tom and I'm an alcoholic, an addict and a adulterer. I'd like to report an infringement by Emily.'

Emily's head shot up, her cheeks reddening, Tom continued:

'She bribed the cook to bring her in chocolate.'

Alan's eyes were bright; he said,

'Thank you, Tom. Emily, how do you plead?'

Emily didn't answer and he barked,

''Fess up, you piece of trash.'

Emily began to cry and he started to clap his hands, said,

'Together, people.'

The group began to clap. Then he stopped, said,

'Emily, did you share this… treat with anyone?'

She shook her head and he said,

'Cat's got her tongue. Well, let the cat keep it. Nobody is to speak to her for three days. Understood?'

'Yes, Alan.'

In unison.

Now he turned to Falls, said,

'And what have we here? Ms Falls, I believe.'

Falls eyeballed him and she could see the smile begin to form on his lips. He turned back to the group, said,

'People, what we have here is a junkie, a thief… and a whore.'

Falls hit him on the side of the head, a Brant special. The closed fist to the top of the ear with maximum force. Then she got up and, with her right hand, grabbed his hair, said,

'Nobody, and I mean fucking nobody, calls me a whore.'

With her left hand, open palmed, she slapped his face four times, leaving fingermarks on his cheeks, said,

'Now that is an infringement. I want you to apologise to Emily, to me, or I'll tear your fucking head off.'

She turned to the group, asked,
'All right, people?'
They roared:
'All right, Falls.'

*I can't stay home. I decide to go to the drop zone
and do a jump, hear all the talk, survive it, or
give myself up. I want the fear of death. I want
to feel those last few seconds, to let fate have
another chance at me.*

Vicki Hendricks
Sky Blues

FALLS AND NELSON were sitting in the car, outside Fern House. Her packed bag was in the back seat; he was trying to suppress a grin, went,

'So you whacked him pretty good?'

'Up the side of the head.'

He paused, then:

'Always the best place.'

She'd expected him to blow, his reaction now was a complete surprise. She asked,

'They wanted me out?'

'And fast.'

'So what now, jail?'

He reached behind the seat, took out a parcel, said,

'For you.'

'A present?'

'Yeah, I guess.'

Unwrapping it, she saw a heavy wooden frame, the dark wood gleaming. Inside the frame was a sign that read:

Tuesday's special
Toad-in-the-hole.'

He smiled, said,

'To tell the truth, the guy didn't want to part with it. Said the sign had been in the window since Romero's opened. I didn't really want to know how long that might have been.'

She took a deep breath, then:

'So, now what?'

'Well, I better get you home and maybe, you'll ask me in for a drink.'

'Okay.'

As he put the car in gear, he said,

'I thought we might... try... and start over.'

She didn't answer for a long time till,

'I don't know if there's such a thing as second chances. It's hard enough first time.'

He tried to keep the disappointment from his voice, said,

'Yeah, I thought I'd ask is all.'

She punched his shoulder, said,

'Jeez, don't give up so easy, where's your fight at?'

Later, that night, lying in bed, he said,

'That was awesome.'

'It's rehab, makes you hot.'

She got out of bed, went to the kitchen, got two beers. The thought of a fast line surfaced but she bit down hard, went back to the bedroom. He was propped up on one elbow, said,

'I better tell you what's been happening with The Blitz.'

'They've caught him?'

'Not exactly.'

He went over the whole series of events and she didn't once interrupt. He concluded with:

'Weiss is holed up in some posh London hotel with *The Tabloid* picking up the tab. Any day now, we'll be treated to his exclusive story.'

Falls put her beer down, said,

'You seem certain he's the killer.'

'Not just me. Brant, Porter Nash, the Kensington guys, they all swear he's the one.'

They were silent and he said,

'Lots of loose talk about someone maybe doing the job themselves, shooting the fuck.'

She was shaking her head, going,

'No, no.'

He shrugged, said,

'I suppose you're right. A cop taking the law into his own hands isn't exactly the ideal solution.'

She took his face in her hands, looked right at him:

'You misunderstand. I'm not against that; it's the shooting I disagree with... it should be a hammer.'

MCDONALD WAS WAITING for Roberts. He thought about what the Chief Inspector had said.

'We've solved the murder.'

He had run it through a hundred times. If Roberts suspected it was McDonald, then he'd already be sitting in a cell. So, someone else, by some bizarre turn of events, had found themselves in the frame. Roberts had laid the killing on another. McDonald asked himself,

'Am I going to let some poor bastard take the rap for me?'

He was already afraid of the answer. Before he could torture himself further, Roberts arrived, said,

'My office.'

They went in and Roberts said,

'Shut the door.'

His desk was cluttered in papers. He moved them aside, said,

'Bad news.'

McDonald figured it was to do with his suspension. He was almost relieved his punishment hadn't been reversed. Roberts continued:

'The murder, I was sure I'd solved it. A friend of the dead man looked set for it: he owed him money, was seen arguing with him, but it turns out he has an alibi. I checked and it holds up. Solving that case would have done us a lot of good. I'm sorry.'

'Sorry?'

'Yeah, I got your hopes up and I know it was personal for you. We'll keep the case open but it's looking like one of those random things and they're the hardest.'

'Yes, sir.'

McDonald tried not to let the relief show; he wanted to cheer. Roberts looked at the pile of files, said,

'We've plenty to keep us busy, though. How about you nip along to the canteen, get us a couple of teas.'

En route, McDonald met the desk sergeant, who went:

'You're looking remarkably cheerful.'

'Just doing the best I can, sarge.'

The guy stared at him, asked,

'Didn't you get suspended?'

'I sure did.'

He moved past and tried to keep the grin off his face. The sergeant watched him go, muttered,

'The new breed, what a bunch of tossers.'

THE INTERVIEW

THE TABLOID
Exclusive interview with Barry Weiss
The man falsely accused of being 'The Blitz'
by
Harold Dunphy

Below the headline was a photo of Barry, looking pensive, as if the world had grievously wronged him. A smaller photo of Dunphy was at the top of the page, looking simply furtive.

The highlights of the exclusive went like this:

'Let me ask you straight out, Barry. Are you The Blitz?'

'No way.'

'Could you be more emphatic?'

'I'm not The Blitz.'

'Why did the police arrest you?'

'Harold, I can understand their desperation. It's a high profile case and they were desperate.'

'But why you, Barry. Why did they pick you?'

'I recently moved to Bayswater and, as we know, a young policeman was tragically killed in Hyde Park. I moved from south-east London, where a policeman was killed and like... *duh!* ...they join the dots. It's regrettable but, on one level, almost comprehensible.'

'How were you treated?'

'Alas, Harold, loath though I am to voice it, I was brutalised.'

'Could you be more specific?'

'They beat me... continuously.'

'And you are taking legal action?'

'Reluctantly. It goes against my most basic beliefs but lest another unfortunate should fall prey to what happened to me, I feel this action will ensure that the police are policed – if I might coin a phrase.'

'The police to be policed, I like it. What now for Barry Weiss?'

'I'm writing a book.'

'I must say Barry, you seem remarkably free of bitterness.'

'I'm not the type to hold a grudge. My personal philosophy is that you pick yourself up, dust yourself down and move on. If I might quote from *Desiderata*: "You are a child of the universe, no less than the trees and the stars, you have a right to be here".'

'Thank you, Barry. Good luck with the book.'

THE INTERVIEW WAS read by every cop in the city. Read and dumped.

A cop went into a hardware shop at the Elephant and Castle, bought nails, a screwdriver, paint and a heavy silver hammer with a black flexigrip handle. The other stuff was just cover – the cop only wanted the hammer.

❐

Two nights later, Barry was still at his plush hotel. He was enjoying the benefits of fame. Drinking in the hotel bar, people had been staring and he acknowledged them with a self-depreciating smile. He'd practised it in the mirror, felt it displayed not only his magnetism but a wedge of humility. He'd downed at least half a dozen scotches – no more shitty lager from now on. When he got his key from reception, the girl gave him a warm smile. He figured he'd take a run at her tomorrow night. For now, he crinkled his eyes, let her juice on that. Along the corridor, he stumbled twice, said,

'Whoops, fellah! Steady on there.'

He was figuring on calling room service, ordering one of those steak sandwiches – and *hey!* – maybe a bottle of champers. Why the hell not, push the envelope out?

Maybe get hold of the night porter, get him to send a little action up. Took him three attempts to open the door. Finally tumbled in, was trying to remember where the light switch was, when an almighty blow crushed his right knee. As he fell back, the light went on. Through the pain, he gasped:

'You!'

The cop swung again and took out most of Barry's front teeth. Barry tried to crawl towards the phone and the cop walked alongside. Barry, through his ruined mouth, spluttered,

'You're...'

The hammer came down again.

Maxwell's
Silver
Hammer

PORTER HAD TAKEN a table at the back. To his surprise, Brant had volunteered to buy the drinks. He arrived with a tray, a mess of pints and shorts. Porter asked,

'Are we expecting company?'

'Just you and me, bro'.'

Porter was going to object, then thought: The hell with it. Took a pint, drank deep.

Brant smiled, said,

'See, you needed that.'

Porter took the shot glass, drained that and Brant said,

'Whoa, give me a chance to catch up.'

Porter reached into his pocket, took out a book, laid it on the table.

Ed McBain

The old Penguin edition.

Brant asked,

'Did you read it?'

'No, it didn't seem appropriate.'

'But you miss the point, Porter. McBain is always appropriate.'

Porter eyed him and Brant said,

'Why don't you just spit it out.'

'What?'

'Did I do it? Did I off that piece of shit?'

'Did you?'

'No, but I have my suspicions about you.'

'I didn't do it.'

Brant finished a pint, belched, asked,

'So, let's say we're both innocent. Then who?'

'Half the Met are suspects.'

Brant raised his glass, said,

'Good riddance to bad rubbish.'

Porter didn't drink, said,

'McDonald was acting very strange. Told me he'd like to do Weiss himself.'

Brant thought about it, said,

'No, he hasn't the bottle. Whoever used the hammer almost demolished old Barry's head. It was close work, real in close and personal. McDonald might be angry but he hasn't that rage, yet. Give him a few more years.'

Porter took another pint, could feel the drink easing him down, asked,

'You think they'll get somebody for it?'

'Let me put it this way, I don't think they'll bust their balls.'

FALLS WAS HAVING a bath, shouted to Nelson:

'Fix yourself a drink, I'll be a while.'

'Okay.'

He noticed the sign he'd given her was lying on the table and figured he'd hang it for her. Went into the kitchen, rummaged in some drawers and found a decent-size nail. Now for something to hit the nail with. Looked round to no avail, saw the cupboard under the sink and hunkered down, opened it. A hammer, with a black flexigrip handle, was lying on a cloth. Pieces of hair and gore still clung to the head.

Falls shouted:

'Hon', you want to scrub my back?'

He stared at the weapon for a few minutes then shouted,

'Just coming, love.'

And shut the cupboard door.